Death Wakes a Snake

A Taylor Texas Mystery

VIKKI WALTON

Morewellson, Ltd.

CHAPTER ONE

Christie laid on the horn. "Can't you see I'm driving here?" The person who'd switched lanes, almost hitting her truck in the process, sped up. She needed to calm down. The last thing she wanted was to have a wreck on her way to get Orchid.

Orchid's calls to Christie were often different. But this call had been unlike any that she'd ever received from the feisty seventy-year-old. It was a simple request.

"Can you come get me?" The emotion had been thick in her voice as she spoke.

Christie replied, "Of course. Where are you?"

"Oh, hun . I'm at home. But, well, there's been a bit of a bother here. You recall that storm we had earlier? Turns out some lines were damaged, and it broke off a large tree branch which hit the gazebo. From there, it took off part of the structure, causing damage to the concrete slab.

And, well, that's when they found them."

"Them?" Christie replied.

"The bodies."

~~

The trip from Comfort had felt like an eternity as Christie finally made it to Orchid's street. Though she wouldn't be getting close to her friend's house. At least not in the truck. A police cruiser blocked the entrance to the street, the lights flashing. She would have to get in from the other side, so she drove on down the road until she could turn into the neighborhood.

Taking a left and then another left, she was met with another police car blocking the street. Various trucks and cars, all displaying signage, were parked up and down the street. Already, people from the next block had gone down to where the police officer had set up a barricade closer to Orchid's house. Christie found a spot to park and exited the truck. She walked back across the street to where a bunch of people congregated and a news team had set up, with a reporter readying to go live.

Wow. News had traveled fast. She walked past the crowd and on toward Orchid's house. Orchid was being escorted outdoors by a young woman who carried a suitcase in her left hand while supporting Orchid's arm with her right hand. It was as if Orchid had shrunk in stature from the load of what had happened.

Tears sprang to Christie's eyes as she sprinted over to her friend. She waved. "Orchid. I'm here."

The no-nonsense woman supporting Orchid appraised Christie with a steely look. "Are you family?"

Orchid grinned. "Don't fret. She's every bit as much family as my real family. Oh darling, are you okay?"

Leave it to Orchid to ask if she was okay. "Yes, of course. I'm just worried about you. It's not every day you get that kind of phone call."

The woman walked Orchid to a chair that had been placed nearby for her. Once she'd settled in, she faced Christie.

"Sorry, I should have introduced myself. I'm Christie Taylor. A friend of Orchid's."

"Amy Calhan. I work with the investigation team who will be handling this case."

Christie gazed at the woman beside Orchid, willing her to give more information. Thankfully, the woman obliged.

"Workers had been doing repair work in the backyard when a large slab of concrete broke loose and took the gazebo with it. As crews were cleaning out the debris, one noticed something shiny in the dirt. He went down to look and found it was a ring."

Christie felt confused. Finding a ring shouldn't have caused all this. "They found a ring?"

Amy continued. "It was on a finger. They called the police who came out, and the forensics team has uncovered two bodies at this stage. That's all I can say at this time."

Christie shot a glance toward Orchid, whose gaze was fixed on the group down the road. It was funny how you could almost lose control in those moments. Christie had done it occasionally, staring at someone or something, unable to look away. She turned back to the woman. "How long before Orchid can return to her home?"

"I'm not sure. Someone from the department will be in contact with her. We've asked that she stay close in case we have questions, but I can't give a time frame."

"If you don't mind me asking, that gazebo has been there ever since I've known Orchid. And probably much longer. You don't suspect her of any involvement, do you?"

"We don't comment on those issues, but from preliminary reports, these bodies have been there for decades."

"Decades." Christie knew that would be good news for Orchid, as she hadn't lived in the house for that long.

"Anything else?" The woman cocked her head, her eyes squinting at Christie.

She realized Amy Calhan had been assessing her while they'd spoken, and would hate to be in her crosshairs. Her strong stance, muscular body, and her tight bun gave the impression that she didn't take guff off anyone. She could probably take down a burly suspect with ease.

"Well, thanks. I'll get Orchid to the hotel now." She made to move when Amy replied.

"What was your name again?"

"Christie Taylor." She watched as the woman appeared to do some mental gymnastics.

Finally, she replied. "Oh, yeah. That's why your name is familiar. When my mom passed, you brought a pie up to the church. That was one of the best pies I've ever tasted."

~~

Christie settled Orchid into her hotel room before leaving. Christie offered to grab Orchid something to eat and bring it back. But Orchid's slack expression and decline of food made Christie realize the incident had affected the usually happy woman.

"Thanks, sweetie. I'm not hungry right now. I was on the phone to my sister when this all happened. She's going to be coming soon to be with me."

"I'm happy to stay here with you or to hang out here."

Orchid patted Christie's hand. "You're a sweetheart. But you're a busy lady. I can't impose on you."

"You'd never be imposing on me."

Orchid's chin trembled. "You're such a good woman, Christie. I'm blessed to have you in my life. Now you go on. This has sapped my energy, and I may take a nap."

"Okay, but don't hesitate to call me if you need anything. I'm not that busy to take care of my friend. Now, let me help you over to the bed." She pulled down the covers and grabbed a water bottle and glass from a tray on a credenza. "Okay, have a good nap. And if you need anything, I mean it, you call me." She bent and gave Orchid a hug before exiting the hotel room.

As Christie took the stairs down to the main floor, she decided to pop in and grab a latte to go. When she'd had her drink, she made her way through the lobby as her phone rang. She looked at the screen. It was Lana.

"Hiya."

"Hey, where are you? I stopped by the office,

and they said you'd left in a big hurry. Everything okay?"

Christie spied a secluded corner and made her way toward it. She settled into a cushy chair. "Yes, sorry. I didn't mean to scare anyone. I'd gotten a call from Orchid to come get her, so I left. Did you need anything in particular or were you just wanting to chat?"

"Ah, okay. I wanted to talk about the latest mare that's come in." Lana was the vet for the equine rescue center, and she was a huge blessing to all the horses that made it to Horse Haven.

"Okay, shoot." She sipped at the latte, allowing the warmth to settle her.

"Nah, we can talk later. Is Orchid's car broken?"

"Well, I'm sure it will be all over the news soon, but they found two bodies, basically sounds like two skeletons, in her backyard."

"You don't say!"

"Yes, I do say."

"Oh, my gosh. And to think I lived right across the street. It gives me the shivers."

When Christie had first met Lana, she lived across the street from Orchid with her kids and folks. So much had changed since then. Now Lana felt like the sister Christie had always wanted. As an only child, Christie had grown up independent, and she still had many of those traits, but she had softened in the last few years. Part of that was because of Lana and her kids.

Lana continued, "So they think that someone that lived here before killed them?"

"No clue. Of course, they weren't saying much right now, but if you lived there, it wouldn't make much sense to do something like that. Not that I would know how killers think."

"I don't know, if anyone would, I think you would."

"Um, excuse me?"

"I'm just saying. You have had experience with them, that's all. Not that you think like a killer."

"Oh, okay. I guess." Christie chuckled.

Lana continued, "Poor Orchid. How's she holding up?"

"She's doing okay. Shaken, of course. She's checked into a hotel, and her sister is flying out to be with her. She's supposed to arrive later. I offered to pick her up, but Orchid said they'd handle it."

"Well, let me know if there is anything that I can do. I can't imagine having something like that happen where I live."

Christie decided not to bring up the fact that they had found a body on the property where Lana lived. Lana had probably forgotten. Better keep it that way. Christie took another sip of the coffee, hoping it wouldn't keep her up tonight. She'd already had a ton of caffeine today. She sighed. "Well, if I find out anything more, I'll let you know. And we can chat about that mare tomorrow if that works."

"Sure. Hey, listen, the kids are both off to activities, want to catch a movie? Say tomorrow around two?"

"Sure. That sounds good. I could use a bit of getting out. It's been a while since I've gone to the movies."

"Anything in particular you want to see? I have one I want to see—"

"Let me guess, a rom-com."

"You know me too well. But there's also a thriller playing around the same time and a drama, if you'd prefer."

"Nah, you pick since you asked me, but expect the rolling of my eyes on some scenes." She laughed.

"I'm going to make a romantic out of you yet."

Christie replied. "Don't hold your breath on that."

"Okay, gotta go. I'll text later with the deets." Lana ended the call.

Christie placed her phone back in her pocket. Sipping her coffee, her mind went to the tragic discovery.

Who had killed the two individuals? But more importantly, who were they and how had they ended up under the gazebo?

CHAPTER TWO

The following morning, Christie checked in on Orchid. During the call, Orchid shared that her sister would arrive later. Orchid wanted her to meet Christie. They decided they'd meet that evening for dinner. Christie said goodbye and ended the call, happy that Orchid sounded better.

The morning was full of potential. Christie had slept well and woken with energy. So she decided to clean the house now to free up the weekend. Turning on some classic country music, she stripped the sheets off the bed. After putting the linens in the wash, she turned to dusting. But as she did the mindless work, her thoughts drifted to the people buried in Orchid's backyard.

According to Amy, they hadn't been recent deaths. But that made it even more curious. Someone had to have been looking for them. And since they were found not that far from the surface, they weren't that long ago either. If not for the cable needing to be updated and the concrete breaking, they probably would have been buried there for decades more.

One thing was sure. They had probably lived somewhere in the area. She tried to remember anything about missing persons cases. If the bodies were decades old, that would have been in their teens or twenties. Christie had left right after high school to attend college. From there, she'd moved to start her internship. And while Pop hated that she hadn't come home, the internship brought a connection with the job she took. It had been her efficient and calm manner that had one of her supervisors recommending she consider hospice care. While Christie had enjoyed being a nurse when she was younger, she was glad those days were behind her.

Something niggled at Christie's mind. But she couldn't quite catch it. Well, it would come to her at some point, but not at two in the morning, hopefully. The morning flew by, and the house was in great condition when she stopped to take a break. She picked up her phone and called Pop.

His raspy voice came through the speaker,

"Hiya, girlie. What's well in your world?"

"Everything Pop. Hey, I'm going with Lana to the movies this afternoon and then out to dinner this evening. Would you like me to bring something home for you?"

"Nah. They're having a potluck at the church, and you know how that goes, all the ladies feel that I can't fend for myself. I'll have enough leftovers for the next week, if not two!" He guffawed.

"Pop, you're terrible."

"Nah, just smart, that's all. You have a good time and say howdy to Miss Orchid for me. Now, why did you really call me?"

Pop had always been a straight shooter and could always hear that something was on her mind just by the tone of her voice.

"I don't know if you heard, but they found at least two bodies over at Orchid's yesterday."

"Ya don't say."

"Yes. You remember that bad storm? Well, it caused some damage to a tree that ended up taking out part of Orchid's gazebo. It also affected some wiring or something in the neighborhood. So workers went in and a piece of the concrete broke off. When they were fixing it is when they found the body. But they think it's probably two, maybe more."

"Well, if that ain't plumb horrible for Miss Orchid. How's she faring?"

"As well as can be expected in the circumstances. It was the first time I'd ever seen her as frail looking as she looked yesterday."

"That's too bad. Now I know what you're thinking—"

Christie laughed, "Oh, do you? And what would that be?"

"You want to find out who they are, don't cha? That way, you can bring closure for Miss Orchid and whoever they found."

"Pop, you know me too well. But there's not much I can do now. I don't have to worry that they'll consider Orchid a suspect. At least I don't think so. But there's something about this that keeps niggling at me. I can't quite put my finger on it."

"Hmm, well, I can chew on it a bit and see if my mind comes up with anything. It takes a while for this brain to cooperate some days."

"Pop, you're blessed that you are still good in that department. But are you taking those supplements I bought you?"

"Those things are big enough for the horses."

Christie sighed. "So no then. Let me see what else I can find, and I'll get those from you. Pop, I want to have you around for a long time, so you have to take care of yourself."

"Hun, I want to be around as long as I can, but you and I know that our days are numbered. So best enjoy 'em while they're here. I'm sure that what you told me will be all the talk at the potluck. So I'll keep my ears open and get back with you on any news."

"Appreciate it. See you tomorrow. Love you. Bye." Christie ended the call.

The rest of the morning, she finished her chores, making her bed with the nice clean sheets. Spritzing lavender on her pillows, she opened the windows to allow a bit of fresh air inside. She sighed with contentment. There was just something about a clean, orderly space.

Glancing at the clock, she decided to take her shower. That way, she could let her hair dry naturally. With her recent cut, the curls had sprung back and, with a bit of goop in her hair, they held their own. It seemed more and more that she found her hair color mixed with strands of silver. Pop wasn't the only one who needed to take care of themselves.

"Pop's right. All we can do is live our lives now and enjoy each moment. And at this moment, it will be enjoying a nice, warm shower."

After she'd showered and dressed, she still had a bit of time left, so she pulled down her book of recipes. That one woman had said she'd loved her pie, why not see about taking one over to her? If she shared any updates with Christie, it would just be in passing. Christie flipped through the pages, her mind on what type of pie would be best received and able to work for them.

But she'd look at that later. For now, it was time to head down to the movie theater. She gathered up her purse and keys, pushing her feet into her new cowboy boots. These were brown with a burnished gold trim and she had fallen in love with them the minute she'd seen them. She'd once read that if you aren't matching clothing to your shoes that you should match your hair color with your shoes. It supposedly gave a finished look of bookending top and bottom. Whether or not it was true, she decided to give it a try with these boots.

To avoid driving back to Comfort before meeting Orchid and her sister, she put on a broomstick skirt, a multi-colored top, and a large woven belt. Her makeup was simple with a good facial oil, color sticks and a quick brush of mascara. She finished it with lip gloss.

Christie made her way down the steps to where the truck's engine already hummed. When she bought this recent vehicle, she made sure it had a self-starter to get the air conditioning going before she had to climb in. Over the summer, it had saved her from entering what felt like an oven.

The drive into Boerne would take some time, so she'd left a bit early. With continued construction all around IH-10, she wouldn't have to worry about being late in case of traffic. But when she pulled up at the movie theater, she found she still had fifteen to twenty minutes before Lana arrived.

Deciding to wait inside, Christie made her way from the truck into the cooler theater. In the past, gatekeepers would often check your ticket. But this newer theater had incorporated the tickets with refreshments. People could go there to check in or buy their tickets, and it most likely was enough incentive to buy a drink or something to eat.

Christie noticed a small stool behind the original ticket counter. Glancing at her phone, she knew it would still be awhile before Lana showed up. She might as well take advantage of the seat. She sat down to wait.

In a moment, a group of elderly ladies came through the door. One holding onto her walker glanced up at Christie.

"Hello there." The woman smiled at Christie.

"Hi," she responded.

"We're here for the movie. She has our tickets." She motioned to another woman, who was fumbling inside her purse.

Deciding it would be easier to give directions, Christie motioned toward the refreshment counter. "You go there, and they'll take your tickets and check you in."

"Thanks, dear." The woman and her entourage shuffled off toward the counter.

Arriving just after them, another couple entered. Younger than the first group, the woman held up her phone screen to Christie. Christie repeated the directions, waving toward the refreshment counter.

This continued on for a few more couples and individuals coming through the door and seeing Christie sitting at the ticket booth. When the last couple approached her, she'd finally decided to say something.

"I don't work here. But if you go over to the counter, they'll check you in." The woman nodded, and the man followed her.

Just then, Christie spied Lana coming through the door. She greeted her, rising from her seat. They went up and stood behind the couple Christie had just advised.

The young woman turned and spoke to Christie. "I see they let you off."

"Yes, and let me tell you, they don't pay all that great either." They all laughed and Christie explained to Lana what had occurred.

They found their seats and settled in for the movie. As much as Christie loved popcorn, she'd forgone it, as she'd wanted to be hungry for an earlier dinner with Orchid and her sister.

The movie was cute, and Christie laughed in spots and teared up in others. In her opinion, that run of emotions was always a sign of a good movie or book.

They'd gone outside after the movie, and Christie took her phone off airplane mode. A message pinged. It was from Orchid.

"I have news."

CHAPTER THREE

After learning that she was with Lana, Orchid invited her to join them as well. When they arrived at the restaurant, they walked in together. A well-dressed woman rose and greeted them with a large smile. "You must be Christie. I've heard so much about you."

"Yes, nice to meet you—"

"Lily."

Christie remembered that Orchid had said her siblings had names of various flowers. "Lily, sorry you had to come visit our area for such a terrible reason."

The woman nodded. "It's a sad state of affairs, to be sure."

Lana chimed in. "Do I detect a northern accent?"

Lily nodded. Her brown eyes sparkling as she smiled again. "Yes, Boston area. I don't hear it that much anymore, but I gather it may sound more pronounced here against your Texan accent."

Orchid was speaking to the hostess, giving Christie a chance to speak to Lily.

Christie lowered her voice, "How's Orchid doing?"

"Certainly, it was a big shock to find out that there were bodies in the backyard. But she's holding up okay. Ah, here she is now."

Orchid walked over and hugged Christie, and then Lana. "Thank you for coming."

"Thank you for inviting me. I would probably be trying to figure out what to pull from the leftovers in the fridge. When I don't have to cook for the kids, I don't do it for myself either." Lana laughed.

"I'm glad you came. And know that it's my treat. I love being around you young people."

Christie chuckled to herself. Only Orchid would consider her forty-plus years as being young. But she'd take the compliment. She was champing at the bit to find out what news Orchid had when the hostess came to escort them to their table. It would have to wait.

After everyone perused the menu, they ordered drinks and entrees. Christie asked Lily. "Was your trip getting here okay?"

"Yes, it was fine. I took a taxi out from the airport, and we have adjoining rooms, so that works well for us."

Christie took a sip of her water after the server placed the cool goblet in front of her. "I would have come and picked you up. You didn't need to take a taxi."

"That's very kind of you to offer. I wasn't sure when I'd arrive, and it was easy to grab a taxi at the airport. No point in putting you out in having to come pick me up."

"It's no trouble. Orchid, do I need to bring your car to the hotel?"

"Way ahead of you. We took care of that this afternoon. That's when I found out the news."

"Yes?" Christie leaned forward.

"They've determined it's only two bodies. I'm at least grateful that it isn't more. And from what I overheard, they may know who they could be."

"Really? Did you find out who?"

Orchid frowned and shook her head. "Sadly, no. I think they'll be clearing out soon, though. They think I can return to the house in a few days. But I'm just not sure."

"What do you mean?"

"That back area had become such a refuge for me, and the gardens were a bit of solitude. Now it will be hard to sit in that gazebo and not think of those two poor souls lying there all this time. I don't know if I can ever go back."

"Oh, no—" She was cut off from saying more when a waiter placed a salad in front of her. Warm rolls with curls of cold butter shapes were passed amongst the group.

Lana slathered the butter on a roll before taking a bite. "Oh, this is divine."

Christie glanced over at Lily, whose gaze was focused on Orchid. Did she see how frail Orchid looked too? Had this tragedy taken a bigger toll than she thought? She said, "But what about your house? Will you sell it?"

"Oh, it's not my house." Orchid wiped her lips with the cloth napkin.

"No? All this time, I thought it was. I mean, you're decorating the front door all the time, and the work you do in the back. I guess I just assumed it was yours."

"When I first moved here, I wasn't sure I would stay. So I rented this place, and just never got around to finding another place. I am—was—content there. But it's time to move on. This is yet one more sign that it's time."

Christie caught Lily's eye. Was there something else that wasn't being shared? Why would Orchid stay in a rental all these years instead of buying her own place?

Her thoughts were interrupted when the waiter removed their salads, but not before Christie noticed that Orchid had barely touched hers. A few minutes later, plates were set in front of them, with each dish looking more delicious than the last. After taking his leave, a quiet descended at the table as they took their first bites of the meal.

"This is delicious. Great choice to come here, Orchid."

"I'm glad you like it." She reached over and squeezed her sister's hand. "And I'm so happy you're here. That's the best thing of all."

Christie almost teared up at the blatant display of sisterly love. To have someone that had known you forever, who could share your blessings and sorrows, was a true gift. She wondered what Orchid would do now, but she didn't want to focus only on the tragedy. Instead, she asked Lily about her life in Boston. Lily regaled them with stories about her two pups at home and then asked about Christie and Lana's work at the equine rescue. Christie let Lana take the lead, and her enthusiasm held Lily's attention.

Lily listened intently. "That sounds wonderful. Before I leave, I'd like to make a donation to your nonprofit. It sounds wonderful."

"We'd be grateful for that. Now, have you been here before? If not, we should take you down to the Riverwalk."

Lily replied, "What's that?"

"It's in downtown San Antonio. There are lots of restaurants along the river, and it's nice for strolling along as well. Or if you prefer to stay up here, we can show you around up here. Or even head over to Fredericksburg for a day trip."

"Can I take a rain check for now? My main priority is my sister and helping her navigate these choppy waters."

"Certainly." Christie replied. "And know that we're here for whatever you or Orchid need."

"I'm ready for dessert!" Orchid chimed in.

Christie saw that most of the food on Orchid's plate had simply been moved around versus eaten. But she remained silent. This incident was taking its toll on the woman. Christie shot up a quick prayer for her friend's well-being.

As the server brought out dessert menu offerings, Christie was going to bypass it, but Orchid and Lily's chiding finally broke her down. The chocolate surprise sounded too good to miss. They all ordered decaf coffee except for Christie. To her, that was like drinking coffee-flavored water, though she'd probably regret it later if she had a hard time falling asleep.

The meal was one of the best she'd had in a

long while, and Christie had enjoyed hearing stories of Orchid and Lily's time growing up. Their stories had the table laughing at their childhood antics and teen crushes. Lana joined in with some stories, as did Christie, and before long, the table was filled with their laughter.

"I hope they don't kick us out for being loud," Lana said.

"I think it's okay. The conversations at the other tables aren't totally quiet either." Christie sighed with contentment. "This has been wonderful. Good food, good conversation, and good laughter."

"I agree," said Lily.

The waiter arrived, asking if they required anything else. "No, thank you, son. And please bring me the check," Orchid responded.

Christie knew from the prices that this had been an extravagant and expensive meal. "Orchid, let me pay for part of it."

"Absolutely not." She set her credit card on the table. "Now, if you'll excuse me for a moment, I'm going to go wash my hands."

She rose gingerly and left the table. Christie wondered if she should just pick up the check, but Lily caught her eye. "You don't know, do you?"

"I'm sorry?"

Lily pursed her lips and shook her head. "Not my place to say." When the waiter returned, she handed him Orchid's card.

That was strange. What did Lily mean by that?

But that question would have to wait. Maybe it had been the caffeine, but Christie would only have a short window to speak to that woman police officer again. For now, her mind was on figuring out how to get over there before they left.

Out in the parking lot, they all hugged, and Orchid said she'd let them know what she would decide soon. Lana chimed in with some sound advice. "I almost moved away after everything happened with us. I'm glad I didn't. So if you'll take a word of advice, I wouldn't make any major decisions anytime soon."

"That's great advice, and I will take it into account, Lana. Thank you for being so thoughtful," Orchid replied. She sighed. "Now, you two, safe travels home."

"You too." Christie embraced Orchid and then Lily. "Keep us posted."

"Will do." Lily responded.

"Good night." Lana waved before getting into her SUV and driving off.

Orchid spoke, "I think that whoever is in my backyard, they weren't meant to be there. And that makes me sad."

Christie started at Orchid's statement.

They weren't meant to be there. And that meant only one thing.

Murder.

CHAPTER FOUR

As Christie drove home, she knew she wouldn't have a lot of time to get over to Orchid's house before the technicians left. And while tomorrow was Sunday, they wouldn't take the day off. She would need to get up early and drive over first thing in the morning. But what to make?

As she drove, she listened to the crooning on the radio, and it settled her a bit. But there were too many things that kept bothering her. One was the remark that Lily had said to her. What did she mean that Christie didn't know? Know what?

She certainly couldn't come out and ask Orchid if she was keeping something from her. Certainly Orchid didn't have knowledge about the bodies in her yard.

Or did she?

How long had Orchid lived in that house? It had been quite a long time as she'd made a reputation for always painting her door a different color or adding artwork every month.

Christie had learned about Orchid's nature when she'd been invited inside. Everywhere was art of some form, most done by Orchid or pieces of art that she'd collected. She had sat with Orchid outside, enjoying the beautiful backyard. She could understand why that peaceful feeling would be gone now.

But it begged the question of Orchid's remarks. Did Orchid know more than she was letting on about the buried bodies?

No, it didn't make sense. Especially as Orchid had been visibly shaken by the discovery in her backyard.

For now, she needed to see what she could find out herself. Knowing that the crew would not have plates and forks, Christie's mind sought how to make it easier for them to eat what she brought.

Of course. She batted at the steering wheel. Fried pies. Then she could also bring them some napkins, but they could easily eat them. She'd need to make a quick stop at the grocery store before heading home. She could prep everything tonight and fry them up tomorrow morning.

Arriving at the store, she parked and went inside. Even later at night, the store had people in shopping for the coming week. Christie grabbed a basket, knowing full well she'd never leave with just what she had come in to get. She moved left into the produce section, stopping to grab some salad fixings for the week, along with some ready-made salsas. Then she turned her attention to what she hoped they had on hand. When she spotted the plump fruit, she let out a sigh of relief. Adding a bunch of apricots to a bag, she twisted them shut and added them to her cart.

Now to grab some lemons, too. She went over all the items she needed to make the compote. She would do that tonight and then put the pies together in the morning, so they'd be fresh. While she would normally create her own piecrusts for them, she decided to take the lazy way out and would go grab some cans of ready-made biscuits.

It wasn't long before her basket held quite a few groceries. If nothing else, she would check this off her to-do list and be ahead of prepping her lunches and dinners for the week. She chatted with a few ladies she knew and checked out with a checker who had volunteered out at the rescue.

The girl had her blonde hair swept back into a high ponytail, and Christie heard her speaking with the bagger. Not surprisingly, it was about some boy in her life. Ah, those high school days. So much drama. Christie laughed to herself. Everything was life shattering if you couldn't go somewhere or do something. And that was decades ago. It had gotten worse. Back in her day, they didn't have to worry as much about being seen in the latest clothing or shoes or having the latest technology. Most wore the same clothes and boots they'd worn that morning doing farm chores. Christie was glad those days were over now. She also felt sad for teens growing up in today's social media world.

She set some bags of produce up on the conveyor belt when the girl turned to her with a dazzling smile. "Oh, hi, Miss Christie."

"Hi, Catelyn. I didn't know you worked here now."

"Yes, I'm saving up for a car. My pa says if I

can save up for a down payment and the insurance, then he'll help me get one."

"Sounds like a good plan."

"Yes, but you know they take so much money out of your paycheck?"

Christie laughed. "Welcome to adulting and the wonderful world of ... never mind, don't get me started."

It was a good thing she quit then, as Catelyn's face bore a confused look. She pushed the apricots onto the scale. "Ooh, are you making apricot pie?"

"Yes, I'm making apricot fried pies. But not for the rescue. However, if you let me know the next time you're volunteering, I'll be sure to have some on hand that day."

"That slaps, Miss C!"

Christie had no clue what Catelyn meant, but figured it meant good. Each generation had its own vocabulary, and hers had been no different. She glanced to the male checker, his hair a tangle of curls. One longer piece kept dropping over an eye, and he kept trying to put it in place by lifting his neck backwards. He loaded the basket and

Christie glimpsed his nametag, Kyle.

She said good night and made her way out to the truck, where she unloaded her items. She chuckled under her breath at some of the conversation she'd heard. The core issues of kids today were the same as before, such as wanting freedom, finding love, and dealing with life problems. But it still felt as if they dealt with so much more than she had.

Before she knew it, she was at home, hauling the groceries up the flight of stairs to her front door. The lights that Bryson had installed were a big help for nighttime, and she missed him. He'd gone off to visit family in Alaska and do some fishing. He promised to bring back salmon for her. Yet another reason she would be happy to see him.

Unlocking the door, she set the groceries down before pulling off her boots. Gathering them up, she made her way to the bedroom where she shucked out of her clothes and into some leggings and a football jersey top.

Back in the kitchen, she put away the

groceries, and set up her instant pot to make some rice for the base of her lunches for the week. Since she was already going to be working in the kitchen, she might as well get some of the other items done for the week.

Taking out her cutting board, she cut the apricots open, discarding the pits. She added the sugar, vanilla, lemon juice and water, mixing it into the apricots before putting it on the back burner to cook down. In the meantime, she chopped up veggies to add to her salad. Pulling out containers with lids, she put in a heaping handful of spring greens mixture before adding the veggies on top. Adding a cup of beans to hot water, she let them sit so she could cook them in the instant pot next.

As she stirred the apricot mixture, she thought about Orchid's sister. While Orchid tended to be more avant-garde in her attire, her sister wore an expensive tailored pantsuit. Even though none of her clothing or accessories shouted wealth, it was clear from her attire and demeanor that she had money. She must have come to help Orchid with finding another place. She struggled to think about Orchid in a different environment. People loved driving by the house to see what she'd painted on her doors. And it had almost become a tourist attraction for some. If they were lucky enough to come at the end of the month, they could see that month and next month's door.

Orchid also did her painting at night so that the new door simply "appeared" as the sun's rays hit it in the morning. It saddened Christie that it wouldn't be there any longer. And where would Orchid be able to move to, as so many places had strict HOAs that focused on conformity versus individuality? No, she couldn't see Orchid living in such a place.

Checking on the compote, it was breaking down well. She stirred it and took it off the back burner so it could start to cool down. She closed up the veggie packs, and would add the rice and protein tomorrow. She yawned. Morning would come early.

CHAPTER FIVE

The alarm clock woke Christie before the sun had come up. She wanted to get a jump on making the pies and get them over to Orchid's house as early as possible. Struggling to get out of her bed, she stretched and padded toward the kitchen. Pulling cans of large biscuits from her fridge, she cut them into two before rolling them out to make small circles. Once she had that ready, she added oil to an iron skillet and turned the flame on the burner.

She flipped on the coffeemaker, enjoying the wonderful aroma that filled the area. Turning on her television, she flipped over to where she had a mix of uplifting and praise music on a mix. She hummed and sang along with the first song as she took a spoon from the drawer. Pulling the apricot compote from the fridge, she heated it up a bit first before adding it to the dough. Using the spoon, she added the warmed-up mixture to one side of the biscuit before covering it with the other half of the circle.

Christie crimped the edges with a fork and turned toward the stove to check the oil. Taking a piece of extra dough, the oil sizzled up around it and she turned the heat down to medium. Using a slotted spoon, she gently placed the first group of pies into the oil. While they cooked, she prepared a standing rack with paper towels underneath to catch any of the oil. Soon the first batch was ready to be flipped over, each one a beautiful golden brown. She prepared the second batch, and in a short time, she had batches cooking and others resting on the stand.

Christie knew that allowing them to rest on the stand first would ensure they wouldn't be greasy when they were stored for travel. Finally, the last batch was done and set next to the rest on the counter. She moved the grease to a back burner to cool and set about cleaning up the kitchen. During that time, her mind had been focused on the music and off of the incident at Orchid's. But as she stopped to drink her first cup of coffee, her thoughts returned to the situation.

Who were these people and why had no one

found them before now? Hopefully, they could be identified and get the justice they deserved.

Christie went to get dressed, grabbing jeans and an old t-shirt. She didn't know if they would leave everything in a mess in Orchid's backyard, and if so, she didn't want Orchid to come home to that. If need be, she'd stay and try to make some order of it.

Grabbing up a large cardboard box she'd kept from a run to the warehouse store, she laid down foil first and then topped it with paper towels. Gingerly, she set the warm pies into the box, leaving out some for Pop for later.

Knowing she'd need to leave in the morning, she'd already ensured that the water tank was full and hay available for her horse, Champ. By the time she made it down to her truck, the sun had crept over the horizon. She headed down IH-10 toward Boerne, hoping that she'd picked the right timing for arriving.

As she made her way down Main Street toward her destination, her thoughts went back to Orchid. She hoped Orchid's vague statements, along with her sister's comments, didn't mean that she planned on moving away. Christie valued Orchid's friendship. Even though they were different in every way imaginable, she cherished the friendship. Orchid allowed her to view things from a new perspective. As Christie tended to rely on her logic, Orchid was so much more in tune with the emotional elements that surrounded people.

Thankfully, the street was no longer blocked off, so that Christie could pull up in front of the house. Yellow and black crime scene tape was still affixed to posts and the tree in the front yard. Do not cross made it clear that people were to stay behind that tape.

What if no one was there or she couldn't get their attention? She hoped she hadn't gotten up at o'dark-thirty only to be thwarted. Then her gaze drifted to the front door.

Orchid must have come over last night. In place of the more whimsical artwork that had been there before, a large shape in blue, white, and silver colors now decorated the door. As

Christie stared at it, the shape grew into focus. It was a solitary teardrop. Leave it to Orchid to capture the feelings of so many at this devastating discovery.

A thought came to her. Yes, it was a tragedy, but maybe it would also bring relief. If someone had been missing, this could bring closure to a family. She opened the door and stepped outside just as Amy Calhan came around the corner of the house. Christie grinned. She couldn't have picked a better time to show up. She whispered, "Now you're just showing off, God."

Perfect. She pulled the fried pies from the interior of her truck as Amy stared at Christie.

Christie smiled as she exited the truck. "Hello, remember me?"

"Yes. You're here early." It sounded more like a question than a sentence, so Christie answered it for her.

"You said that you'd enjoyed my pies the other day. I know that the crew is going to be finishing up soon and thought I'd bring these by for you. As you know, my friend, Orchid, lives here and I—." She stopped, realizing she was rambling now. She lifted the kitchen towel that covered the pies so the woman could catch a glimpse.

"Apricot. I knew it would be hard to eat a regular pie, but I figured y'all get to take breaks and these will work for that. They're still warm now but are okay, cold too. In fact, are nice with a scoop of good vanilla ice cream."

Amy put her hand on her chest. "Oh, you're killing me. I've been working since four this morning, and I'm ready for something to eat. May I?"

"Of course. Help yourself. I also brought napkins too. If you don't mind holding this for a minute, I'll grab them from the truck."

The woman took the box while Christie retrieved a plastic bag that had napkins, some hand wipes, and a small container of powdered sugar. She showed the woman the items. "The powdered sugar is for those folks who really like theirs sweet. They should be where they can be dusted. Or people can sprinkle some on the pie after taking a bite."

The woman set the box down on the porch nearby. "The techs are pretty much done, it's mainly paperwork now and just to check everything one more time. So they'll appreciate these."

"Great. I came by for another reason. I don't suppose they'll put things back the way they were. Am I able to go in and try to clean it up a bit before Orchid comes home? Although I see by the front door that she's already been by."

"Yes, she asked permission to repaint her door one last time. She was working on it last night when I came on shift. To be honest, I was a bit surprised they allowed it. But I guess it's because everything is relegated to the backyard." She turned and glanced at the door. "She has a real talent for making art that speaks to your soul."

"That's it exactly. I always feel something when I look at her door. Usually happiness, but she's also made me feel sadness on occasion, just like this time."

Amy bit into one of the treats. Christie waited while she finished the fried pie.

"These pies are delicious. I should take them to the techs in the back so they can grab some while they're still warm." Dusting off her hands, Amy picked up the box and bag.

Shoot. It didn't look like Christie was going to get more information. Oh well. Why hadn't she offered to take them round back?

Amy glanced over at Christie. "You can come with me. At this point, the tape is mainly to keep snooping eyes away from the property. Then they can see who their pie benefactor is."

"Great. Let me carry the box, and that way you can grab another pie."

"Don't mind if I do." Amy took another pie from the box, before transferring the bag into her other hand.

They started toward the back with Christie carrying the box. As they made their way back, she heard voices and the sound of metal on metal. Coming around the back, two people were dismantling a tent.

"I heard that it was only two bodies that were found. Are they able to have an idea about how long?"

A tall, lanky man strode over toward them. "What do we have here?"

"Fried apricot pies." Christie replied.

"That sounds, and smells, great." He tucked a clipboard under his arm as Amy handed him a napkin.

After the team had oohed and aahed over the warm pies, Christie asked, "I don't suppose y'all have any idea on how those bodies ended up in Orchid's backyard?"

Another man, this one much younger, joined them. "There's some possibility that it could relate to a missing person's case in the late eighties or nineties."

The older man bristled. "What did I tell you about saying anything to anyone about this?"

Christie watched as the young man's face turned beet red. "I, um, I thought she was someone on the team."

"Newbies. Don't let it happen again or you're

fired!" He stalked away before turning back and grabbing another of the fried pies.

Christie remained quiet. A cold case. Who had gone missing and why had they ended up here?

CHAPTER SIX

Christie waited as the woman took the new worker aside and spoke to him quietly. He nodded before heading back off to finish deconstructing the tent.

"I guess I wasn't supposed to hear that."

Amy shrugged. "News media have already been by. You know that they're going to be doing some digging into this house and people missing in the past. It's just a matter of time before things come out. And media doesn't care if it's only conjecture. It's news, and they'll put it out there with lots of disclaimers."

"It would make sense that it could be something to do with missing people."

"That's just it. As far as I know, I don't recall any missing persons case, just a missing person." She sighed. "It may not even be related to the bodies discovered here."

"Orchid told me she's been renting this house. Has the homeowner been notified?"

She nodded. "Yes, though it's through a rental company. They have to notify the owner for us."

Christie cleared her throat. "How hard will it be to identify the remains?"

"Well, there was some jewelry they found with the bodies, and of course, DNA identification has come a long way. If there's any match in a database, they can use that."

All of a sudden, a crash startled them. The tent pole had come apart, and the young man was lying in a heap on the ground. Amy sprinted over to help the man along with the older tech lead. Christie moved over to set the box of fried pies down on the table. He'd left his clipboard there, and it was turned to a page of items found next to the skeletons.

Broken necklace one-half mizpah?

Class ring '88 no name/school men's?

The sound of a diesel truck and tires braking came to them. Christie jumped as a man rushed around the side of the house. "What's going on here?"

The main tech lead said, "Sir, you can't be

back here. This is an investigation."

"Investigation? Who gave you permission to be back here?" He gasped at the sight of open ground. "No, no, it can't be." He wailed before his face went pale. He grabbed his chest and slumped to the ground.

Amy rushed over to him as he fell. "Call 911. I think he's having a heart attack." She started performing CPR on the prone man. While they'd been chatting, the sun had risen and now the backyard was fully in light.

Amy stared down at the man as she pumped his chest with her hands. "Mister Friedrichs. Hang in there."

And just like that, the past came rushing forward.

~~

1989

Christie held her hair up as she sprayed it one more time. While lots of the other girls had broken down and got perms, her naturally thick and wavy hair already gave her a lot of volume. She smoothed down her plaid shirt, making sure it was tucked into her blue jeans. Her western belt buckle had a rose on it, and she'd polished it before pulling it through her pant loops. Hooking it into the belt, she did a quick spin in front of the long mirror. Satisfied with her look, she pulled out the box with her new pair of red Ropers. She had finished putting them on when she heard a car pulling up.

"Pop, I'm leaving for school!" The house was small enough she didn't really need to yell, but lately, it seemed like Pop couldn't hear her or had something else on his mind.

Pop was standing in the front doorway, his arms crossed against his chest. "I don't like those two."

"Now, Pop, don't be so gruff." She kissed him on the cheek and grabbed a couple of books and a sack lunch off the nearby table. Hurrying outside, Trish was leaning out of the brown Camaro's window. "Come on, Christie."

Christie turned and waved at her father before Cole opened the driver's side door, pulling the driver's seat forward so she could get in the back.

"Hi, Christie. You, um, look nice today," Cole said.

"Thanks." She bent over to enter the car, catching Trish's hateful facial expression.

Was Trish jealous because he'd complemented her? She sat back as Cole took his time, backing up carefully as Pop watched from the porch. Once they hit the main road, he downshifted before moving through the gears quickly. Christie smiled as she thought it wouldn't be too long before she could get her permit, and over the summer, she'd be taking driver's ed. Then she'd have to convince Pop to let her get a car or take the truck to school.

They pulled up at the school. She noticed a large group of kids standing around talking. The trio made their way over to the group.

"What's going on?"

A girl in an FFA jacket spoke, "Haven't you heard?"

"Stacy Fredrich is missing."

Christie knew the name, as Stacy was the

head cheerleader for Boerne High School.

"What do you mean, she's missing?"

"Her mother and father called the police last night because she never came home."

Trish's voice was excited, "What do you think happened?"

Lots of shrugs in the group. One guy, wearing a beaten-up cowboy hat, pulled a round can from his back pocket before stuffing a pinch of tobacco under his lower lip. He placed it back in the pocket that revealed a white outline of the can. "Heard my folks talking about it this morning. Says she probably done run away. There was a bag of her clothes missing from her bedroom."

Trish spat out. "I'm sure she'll turn up. What's she going to do, anyway? It's only news cause she's head cheerleader."

Christie glanced over at her friend again. Had she always been jealous of others and she was revealing it for the first time? Or had Christie just not noticed it until now? Was there something to what Pop had said earlier?

Christie glanced at her Swatch watch. "Gotta

get to class."

The others nodded, breaking out into solos and pairs of walkers.

She remembered thinking that it would be settled in a few days. But she'd been wrong.

Present Day

Christie waited until the ambulance had left with Stacy's father. Why had he come here this morning? Certainly, they wouldn't have released any information to him yet. The events of the morning were getting stranger and stranger. Leaving the techs to finish their work, she went and sat in her truck, taking time to offer a prayer for Mister Fredrich.

Her thoughts traveled back to the past where the following days after Stacy's disappearance had many parents on edge. A vigil had been held in the Boerne Main Square with her parents in attendance. Both of them looking as if they had aged decades. While there had been some searching, the fact that clothes and a bag were missing from the home, along with personal items, led police to believe she was a runaway.

Stacy's mother stood tall with her father next to her, a shell of the man he'd been.

Irene's face bore a slack expression with wet, dull eyes. Most likely, she hadn't slept all night. Her voice quivered and broke as she spoke. "We know that Stacy would never have run away. Someone, please anyone if you know anything, let us know. We only want Stacy home with us."

Flyers were posted. People searched their properties. False reports were given. But as days turned to weeks and then months, the disappearance of Stacy Fredrich faded into the background of one more sad memory. Many thought she'd run away or gotten involved with drugs. Rumors abounded on what had happened to the popular cheerleader.

It wasn't long until the toll affected Stacy's parents, leading them to separate. Her father had moved out, leaving Stacy's mother at the house they shared. She refused to leave or move, stating that Stacy would come back one day, and she wanted to be there when she did. She was finally diagnosed with lung cancer. Even though Christie had been a nurse, she understood the mind and body connection and how the lungs are associated with grief. But they'd caught it early, so she had kept it in remission. Finally, the couple divorced. By this time, more than a decade had passed, and Irene moved to Florida. Orchid had moved in after that.

If the body they found was Stacy's it would at least bring closure to her parents. But that would only answer one question. Another one remained.

Who was the second person?

CHAPTER SEVEN

A call startled Christie from her reverie. It was Pop.

"Hi, darlin. Are you okay? Missed you at church."

Christie glanced at her phone. The time had flown by since this morning. She let out a sigh. "No. I'm fine. It's a long story, Pop."

"Well, Lana invited us over for Sunday dinner. Do you want me to come pick you up?"

"No. I'm in Boerne. I'll tell you about it when I get there. See you soon."

"Love ya."

"Love you too." She hung up. The love between parent and child was one of the strongest things. She and her father had grown even closer when her mother had passed away when Christie was young. She recalled how they had spoken briefly about Stacy when she'd gone missing. He emphasized the dangers of running away from home, and of course, stranger danger. There had been more, but she didn't recall other conversations about it. Maybe this time she could ask Pop more questions about what went on during that time.

She made it to the Altgelt homestead in good time. She hated that feeling of 'waking up' to find yourself at a spot you'd been driving to. It was as if your mind divided and one part of the brain took over the driving while the other—subconscious mind—went off in its own direction. It was scary because it wasn't something you were aware you were doing.

Christie parked under a tree, but didn't turn off the engine for a minute. She felt unsettled by this morning and by reliving some of her past. She needed a moment to compose herself before she went inside.

She exited the door and spied the dogs, Mutt and Jeffrey, under the large oak. "What are you two doing over here? Did Pop bring you over in the truck?" They thumped their tails but were busy chomping on some treat that Curtis or Lana must have given them.

Striding over to the porch, she opened the front door. She was greeted as soon as she entered the house by the smells of chicken fried steak and fresh hot bread. Lana's daughter, Allie, was setting the table.

"Allie, you are getting so tall. What's your mom feeding you?"

Christie knew that the budding young woman would have the boys eating out of her hand. If they didn't already follow her around. The best thing was that Lana had raised her kids to be good people.

She giggled and set down a plate. "Hey, Miss Christie. I like your outfit today."

"Thanks. Can I help you set the table?"

"I'm about finished, but thanks."

Lana pulled more crispy brown meat from the skillet, placing it on paper towels to get rid of excess oil. That reminded Christie about the fried pies at home. She could have brought some over. Oh well.

"Let me know what I can do to help."

"Nothing right now. Just have a seat." Lana

drew up the pieces of drippings and laid them off to the side. Pouring out most of the oil, she put the crunchy pieces back in the pan before adding some flour. After adding that, she added in a slurry of milk, flour, and a pinch of cornstarch, stirring it into the pan. She added salt and black pepper, continuing to stir it. "Now that I think of it, if you can corral Pop and Curtis, this is ready to eat. I just need to finish the white gravy, and it'll be done by the time y'all return."

"Be happy to help." Christie went out the back door and crossed over to where Pop and Curtis were sitting outside on chairs in front of the tiny home that Curtis now lived in.

Pop rose. "Hey, girlie. I gather it's time to head over for some good grub."

"And you'd be right." She waited as Curtis took a bit longer to get to his feet. "That Lana puts on a great spread. I think I'm needing to loosen a belt notch."

"Curtis, I doubt you weigh one fifty soaking wet. You could use a bit of meat on your bones," Christie responded.

In truth, his health had been going downhill for some years, and having Lana and the kids nearby had brought some new vigor to him.

"Where's your fella?" Curtis inquired.

"Bryson is up in Alaska. He's bringing back some salmon, so we'll share some with you."

He waved a gnarly hand toward her. "I'll stick to my meat and taters. Speaking of which, I see Lana waving at us to come on. So best get to it."

They walked over to the house. Inside, they made their way to the table that was piled high with the prerequisite meat and potatoes. Accompanying the main dishes were creamed corn, green bean casserole, along with macaroni and cheese. There was also a salad along with some jars of homemade pickled okra and pickles.

"I might as well just go to sleep now." Christie laughed.

Lana looked at the food. "I know. It's a lot of carbs, but the kids love having the mac and cheese for afternoon snacks after school."

Christie knew that much of the food was for Pop and Curtis, and she winked at Lana. After

Curtis had said the blessing, they all piled their plates with the delicious food. Christie asked Allie about school, and Lana's son, Trey, shared some of his recent events. Laughter flowed as well as the sweet, iced tea. Before long, everyone had had their fill. The kids were excused, and then the attention turned to Christie.

"So tell us about your morning. I've been dying to find out what went on ever since your dad shared why you weren't at church."

Christie gave them a breakdown of what had happened earlier. "Pop, do you remember when all that happened?"

"Sure do. Even though it wasn't up here, it was close enough that all us parents were keeping a watch on all the kids. I thought maybe she'd taken off. You know, gotten mad at her folks and thought she'd show them, but when she didn't come back, that's when people started getting more worried. Fact is, Stacy was a good girl. No one thought for a second that she wouldn't leave a note for her mama or call. Nope, we all thought something had happened to that young'un. We just didn't know what. So are they thinking it's her they done found?"

"Possibly. But that begs the question of the other body. Did someone kill one person first and then later kill her? I mean, and I hate to think it, but was there a serial killer on the loose back then?"

Pop shook his head. "I think we'd have heard of more young people going missing. Far as I know, she was the only one." He then went on explaining about the events of the time, the media focus on her parents, friends, etc.

"You know, you ought to talk to Susan." Pop said.

Christie wiped her mouth. "Susan?"

Curtis answered. "Susan Furtado. She used to be a librarian, and she'd probably be able to help you find out what you want to know. She's Bryson's cousin."

"I didn't know that. How can I get in touch with her?"

"Hmm. I think she's up in Lawton now visiting family, but she should be back soon. I'll find out from her ma when she'll be back. Or you can probably ask Bryson."

"Sounds good. Now, you two ol' geezers get out of the way so I can clean up these dishes and chat with Lana."

Chuckling, the pair went out the back door to head back over to Curtis's porch.

Lana picked up some plates. "How long do you think before they're both snoring?"

"Five minutes?" Christie asked.

"That long?" Lana replied.

Christie laughed as she picked up the bowl of mashed potatoes. "Why don't you sit down and put your feet up and let me take care of this? After all, you did all this cooking. I can, at least, do the cleaning."

"Well, if you insist." She winked.

Christie laughed. "I do." She created a pile of plates next to the sink and trashcan. She was glad that Lana had gotten a dishwasher installed as that made cleaning up much faster.

Lana shucked off her shoes and put her feet up on a chair she pulled across from her. "Did you know this Stacy person?"

Christie shook her head. "No. Not only did she go to a different school, but she was some years ahead of me. I had just started my sophomore year, and she was starting her senior year."

"Oh, that's even more sad." Lana's voice cracked.

"Yes, and it was interesting what Pop said about her folks. I guess it's normal to try and place the blame on someone. That if they hadn't done something, Stacy never would have left or been lured away."

"Yes, after I heard about the discovery, I was a mother hen to the kids."

"You mean more than usual."

"Yep. Curtis even told me to 'back off' but in nicer terms." She laughed. "I can't help it. Now, when are we going to do our own investigating?"

"Why do you think—"

Lana arched an eyebrow.

"Okay, you got me. You know me too well. I have to find out what I can to satisfy my curiosity.

And who knows, help get Stacy some justice. I mean, are they going to open up a new file on her now? Where would they even know where to look?"

Lana folded her arms. "I'm sure they have some insights. Plus, they do this for a living. Just saying."

"Of course. I guess that didn't come out sounding right. But if we can help them, maybe we can help her father get a bit more closure. He was so distraught this morning. I hope it was just a panic attack versus a full-blown heart attack."

"We could probably stop by and see him tomorrow."

"Don't you have a new patient coming in?"

Lana cleared her throat. "Those two new vet interns can handle it if they bring the ponies before we get back. What do you say? Can you be a bit late into work?"

"I think so. Plus, I want to check in on Orchid again. She repainted her door. It's a big teardrop."

"Aw, leave it to Orchid to know the perfect thing to put there. I'm sure she'll be okay."

"When I spoke to Amy this morning, she said Orchid wanted to do it 'one last time'. I don't like the sound of that. Is she really set on moving out, and if so, is she going to stay here or go with her sister?"

"I hope not. Orchid's such a fun person. I'd really miss her."

"Me too." Christie sighed.

CHAPTER EIGHT

Christie had just walked in the door when her phone rang. It was Bryson.

"Hello, you."

"Hello to you. How's the fishing going?"

"Good. Though I think some of these guys are more into hanging around a campfire and drinking at night."

"Well, it's a good thing they have you there to keep watch and keep them in line. Otherwise, you all might end up as bear catch." She laughed.

"Yep. I'm glad I came. It's gorgeous up here, but I'm missing my beautiful lady."

"Ah, your horse is doing fine here."

"Funny."

Since Bryson was gone, he often popped into her thoughts. "I miss you too. I'll be glad when you're back cause I'm wanting some of that salmon."

"Of course. Why else?" He chuckled.

"Anything exciting happening, or should I not

ask?"

"Probably better to not ask, but I'm going to tell you, anyway. They found two bodies in Orchid's backyard."

"Okay, I wouldn't have come up with that. How—"

"Probably easier if I tell you some facts, and it may answer some of your questions."

"Okay, let me put my feet up as I feel this is going to be some story."

"You could say that. Remember, right before you left, that Orchid had an issue with the gazebo in the backyard? Well, turns out they had to do some work on cable lines or something through her yard, and that's when they found them."

"Wow. So not just in her yard, under her yard?"

"Right. They'd been there for some time. Even before Orchid moved in."

"How's Orchid doing with all this?"

Christie appreciated Bryson and his thoughtfulness in asking about Orchid. "Not so great. She painted a huge teardrop on the front door and said it was the last time. She's not even staying there and not sure she plans to live there anymore after this. Her sister came into town and is staying with her at a hotel in Boerne."

"Ah, that's too bad. Not just for Orchid, but for so many that love her door art."

Christie sat on a chair, pushing off one boot with the other foot. Then doing the other one. She wiggled her toes, enjoying the freedom of being out of the boots. "That was what I thought, too. Quick question. You went to Boerne High School, right?"

"Yes. Why?"

"Well, there's some speculation that one body is a girl who disappeared back in the late eighties or nineties. Does that ring any bells?"

"Um, let me think. Oh, yes. The head cheerleader. Oh man, so she didn't run off."

"They haven't confirmed it yet, but it's a possibility. Do you have your old high school yearbook from then?"

"Yes, I can hunt for it when I get home. Wait until you see me. I look like a true mountain man with this beard and longer hair.”

“Hmm, sounds interesting. Can’t wait to see it. Now, back to the issue here. I feel so sorry for Orchid and for whoever has been hidden all this time. They deserve justice.”

“I agree. And the police will work toward that.”

Christie sighed. She knew that the police were good at their jobs, but she also knew that their plates were overflowing with live cases. How much time would they be able to give to a cold case? “When you get back, I’d like you to tell me what you remember about it and if there was any speculation about any of the people around her once she disappeared.”

“Off the top of my head, I remember that her boyfriend at the time came under a lot of scrutiny. I think Stacy’s dad and he almost came to fists in the parking lot. And then there was the football coach. You know, in today’s culture, he would have been fired or sued with the way he ogled and spoke to the cheerleaders back then. If I had to put my money on anyone, it would have been him.”

"What about her girlfriends? Did they have any ideas about it?"

"I didn't run with that jock crowd, but I know that her best friend left the team after she disappeared, and another girl took over as head cheerleader."

"Hmm. That's motive."

"Really? To become head cheerleader?"

"People kill for reasons that seem baffling to others, but you have to remember you're often dealing with someone who is a psychopath or sociopath. They have no feelings about taking a life if it gets them what they want."

"And you know this how?"

"I read. And watch shows. Plus, when I was caring for some of my hospice patients, you wouldn't believe some people I encountered. Their so-called loving children wanted them out of the way so they could grab their money. The more money at stake, the worse it got. I even thought that one was a reverse-Munchausen case."

"That's horrible. What happened?"

"I notified the doctor, and we made sure that the patient was having a procedure or not alone in the room when her daughter arrived. Of course, after a while, the woman patient started recovering. Of course, this was before lots of cameras and other security measures, so we could never prove anything."

"What happened?"

"Her daughter was involved in a terrible car accident. She ended up in a nursing home herself."

"That's karma for you. What about the old lady?"

Christie chuckled. "She was in better shape than lots of people. She ended up competing in CrossFit challenges and, as far as I know, she's still living life to the fullest. She also decided to spend more of her hard-earned money, and so she and her grandkids were always going traveling together. I still get postcards now and then from the places she's visited."

"So a happy ending, then?"

"Yes. I'm still amazed that people can wish

harm on those in their own family."

"Does that make you think that her parents had anything to do with her disappearance?"

"I can't say. But nowadays, it's that they often look to a spouse or parent if something happens. I don't know enough about them to make any sort of judgement."

Bryson answered, "Well, if you would have seen the way they were afterwards, I doubt you'd even consider them. I'd seen them at the games, and Stacy was their world. When she disappeared, it was like their spirits had separated from their bodies, only leaving a shell of a person."

"That's heartbreaking," Christie replied.

"Yes, I think that's why they ended up divorcing. I don't know if they each blamed the other, or they just couldn't handle the grief."

Christie sighed. "Let's change the subject. This is getting depressing. I'm looking forward to your being home."

"Me too."

"You know, I've never kissed a man with a beard."

"Even more incentive for me to hurry home."

Christie laughed. "Okay, well, let me know when you're coming in. I can drive into San Antonio and pick you up at the airport."

"Okay, love you."

"Love you too."

Christie ended the call, her thoughts on their conversation.

Someone had killed Stacy. Someone she knew and possibly trusted. The question was why.

CHAPTER NINE

Work was busy for the next few days, so it didn't give Christie much time to focus on the deaths. Orchid had taken some time away to think, so she and her sister were heading to the coast for a few days. Christie felt antsy, so that meant she needed to get some physical activity in. She saved the document she was working on and picked up a baseball cap. Pulling her hair into a ponytail, she pulled it through the back open area. On her way out, she stopped to let the new volunteer know that she was heading over to the horse barn next door in case anyone needed her.

Walking over, she waved at the people coming and going. They must be starting an equine therapy class. Inside, she found Lana, who was grateful for Christie's help.

"I could use it. We're shorthanded today. If you could help with walking the horse with the rider around the corral, that would be good. Then a couple of our boarded horses could use a ride if you're up to it."

"Do you even need to ask?" Christie winked before joining staff members and parents who were placing children up on the horses. One child wasn't having any of it.

Christie walked over and bent down in front of the child. "Hi there. I'm Christie. I don't blame you for not wanting to wear those helmets. They make my hair go like this." She mimicked her hair sticking out all over the place.

The child laughed.

Christie lowered her voice. "Can I let you in on a secret?"

The child's eyes grew wide. Looking over to her mother, the mother nodded her consent. "Okay."

"You see Lady, here?"

The child nodded.

"She doesn't like all this stuff on her either. In fact, when we first got her, she would throw a right fit about putting on a saddle or a bit, but look at her now, standing there all pretty-like, just waiting for you."

"She is pretty."

"I'll let you in on another secret. Now that she's used to it, she actually knows that she gets to carry cool people like you on her back."

The young girl clapped her hands.

"But she knows that it's better if you wear this hat on your head. Even if it makes your hair look funny."

"I'm scared," the little girl whispered.

"Well, how 'bout this? Have you been introduced to Lady yet?"

The girl shook her head.

"So, this is your first time here?"

The girl nodded, and Christie stole a glance at the mother. It was evident that she was tired and worried about her child. That may have been part of the child's problem with easing onto the horse.

"Hey, mama. How about you go sit over on that bench? That way you can wave to your kiddo from up higher where she can see you without looking down or around."

The mom's face showed her relief. "That's a great idea. I'll be right over there, honey."

The girl nodded.

"Okay, so ready to give the hat a try?"

She grinned widely, a gap showing where her front teeth were missing. "Yes."

"Great." Christie helped the girl into the helmet, letting her get used to it before closing the buckle. "Well, don't you look all fancy now? Let's go say hello to Lady and ask if she'll be okay with you taking a ride on her."

Christie and the young girl went over to where Lady stood waiting. The mare bent her nose down so that the child could pet its muzzle.

"Her nose is soft. But hard too." The girl giggled when the horse's nostrils moved.

"Yes, a bit like our noses. Now want to help me walk Lady over to the stairs?"

In working with various riders, they had incorporated various ways to mount the horses. One was a staircase that allowed easier access to the horse versus picking someone up to put on the horse. It wasn't long before Christie had the girl settled in the saddle. Another volunteer Christie had called over stood holding the reins until everything was in place. Then Christie went over and walked alongside the girl while the volunteer walked in front with the horse's reins.

"Mommy, Mommy! Look at me. I'm riding a horse." The girl grinned.

"That's wonderful, sweetie." Her mom replied. As they passed by, Christie noted the woman wiping the tears from her eyes.

After they had gone around a few times, they repeated all the steps in taking her off of Lady. "Hey, if you go with Catelyn here, she'll show you how she feeds Lady a treat. She loves apples."

"Okay." The girl placed her pudgy hand in Catelyn's as they moved out of the corral toward the barn. The mother joined Christie.

"I can't believe it. She's probably said more words in the last hour than she has in days. I really appreciate you're letting me see if this would work for her."

"Certainly. Riding will also help with balance and lots of other cognitive issues. I'll be happy to give you some literature for you to take home and see if you'd like to continue the therapy for your little girl."

"That sounds great. Oh, it's my mom. Mom!" She waved at a woman who appeared to be around Christie's age.

The woman walked over toward them. Why did she look familiar to Christie?

"Hi, I'm Joy." She held out her hand to Christie, who took her extended hand.

After a firm handshake, Christie asked, "Sorry, have we met before?"

"I don't think so. But who knows? Sometimes you've seen someone, and it sticks in your mind."

"Yes, I guess. Anyway, it was nice to meet you both. Please let me know if you have questions. I'll be in the neighboring barn before heading out for a ride, but if you are good for now, I'll say goodbye."

"I think I'm good for now. Thanks again. I really think this can help my daughter have more confidence too. Sadly, she has a few kids that bully her at school."

Christie noted the mom's face cloud over.

"I'm sorry to hear that."

"Well, it's not the kids' faults. Most times, the parent's haven't instilled good values. Though when they get older, they have a choice to behave better. Unfortunately, some don't." Joy sighed. "I'm going to wait in the car in the AC. Nice meeting you."

She strode off, leaving an awkward silence between the pair.

"Well, best be off. Again, please call if you have questions. Don't hesitate." Christie walked toward the barn that connected to the secondary outbuilding where they boarded horses for people. Her thoughts drifted to the mother's words about bullying. If anything, you heard of bullies more today than in the past, but was that simply because of social media or were people just becoming less respectful to one another? She didn't know. Thankfully, everyone that worked at the equine rescue were all good people, and there hadn't been any issues on that front that she'd had to deal with.

She smiled as she entered the next barn and saw her horse, already saddled and ready to go.

Exiting the barn, she mounted the Paint, walking over to a large, fenced area. This area had been cleared so that they could let the horses run without the chance of any stray rocks or roots.

She bent over and patted the horse's neck. "You take it from here."

The horse whinnied and before long she was galloping across the field, her thoughts quiet and totally in the moment. After she returned the horse to the barn, Christie was working with the curry comb when Lana came up to her.

"Good ride?"

"Yes, I always feel so much better after a ride. It's a good way to get the lymph system activated for me. I may get a rebounder to put in my office. Sitting down at my desk is really taking its toll on me."

"You could get a standing desk."

"I thought about that, but I need the space to spread out all the paperwork. I guess I need to be more proactive on getting in more exercise."

"You're running around all day."

"Yes, but when I was a nurse, I was on my feet

all day long. Plus squatting, bending, etc. I just want to make sure I stay healthy."

Lana grinned. "You are healthy, but I get it. I'm not a fan of paperwork either. That's why as much as possible, I get the intern vets to do the write-ups, and then I review them. It's saved me a lot of time in front of the computer."

"That's a great idea. Maybe I can figure out what things I can delegate. You know me, though. Delegating is not in my nature."

"Boy, do I. But it will be better for you in the long run. Plus, you'd be able to help me more over here. You did great this morning with that new person coming in to check out the therapy offerings."

"Yes, she also came with her mom. She looked familiar. Did you happen to see her?"

"Sorry, no. I was too busy with the pregnant mare that came in."

"No matter. Probably just reminds me of someone."

"Speaking of someone's, when's Bryson coming home?"

"Soon. I'll be glad he's back," Christie replied.

"I'm sure he'll be glad to be back, too. Now, I best be getting back to work. See ya."

Christie's phone dinged. She reached down and saw a text come through. "Lana, wait."

"What is it?"

"They've positively identified one of the bodies as Stacy Fredrich."

CHAPTER TEN

When Christie picked up Bryson from the airport, she quickly launched into the latest discovery. After hearing the news, she'd gone online to find more details that the police had released. Stacy had been confirmed as one victim, but they were still searching for the identity of the second person. The only thing they'd revealed is that they determined the second person to be a male.

Christie turned on her blinker, merging onto Loop 410. "What do you think? By the way, I like your beard."

He stroked his beard with his right hand. "Thanks. I'm keeping it for now. We'll see if it stays come the heat of next summer. As for your question, if she was with another boy, that could be motive if her boyfriend found out."

"True. But it could also be the boy's girlfriend if she found out."

"I suppose, but I think it would be more difficult to take down two people. I wonder what caused their death."

"Blunt force trauma."

He raised his eyebrow.

"Don't look at me like that. Let's just say that fried pies can get you information if you do it right."

"Or put you in jail."

"Well, that too, but I'm not doing anything with it but telling you." She grinned.

He tapped his fingers on his leg, a habit Christie recognized now when he was thinking. "If they were ambushed, it makes sense why the neighbors may not have heard anything."

"Actually, one house was empty and being remodeled, and the people who owned the house on the other side were out for the evening. But here's the strange thing. The house Orchid lives in now is also the place where Stacy lived for a short time. They were building a house and were renting it until they completed the house."

"Oh, wow. So they moved after that?"

"No, the mom wouldn't leave in case Stacy came back. The dad moved out. From what I've heard, it sounds like their marriage pretty much ended the day Stacy left. Well, you know. Disappeared."

"Well, at least they'll have closure now. Have they said anything about it?"

"Her dad is still in the hospital from the heart attack. He's not making any comment."

"And the mom?"

"She lives in Florida now. I can't imagine how she must feel knowing that her daughter was there all this time."

Bryson nodded. "It's sad, even if it brings closure. At least the other way, they had hope. Listen, I talked with Pop and contacted Susie. She said she'd be happy to help. She's going to bring over the yearbooks so we can take a look at them."

Christie loved that Bryson and Pop had such a great relationship. It made her feel good that the two men respected each other and enjoyed each other's company. "Great. I have to get back to the rescue to finish up some paperwork. What time should I stop by?"

"Come whenever. I told her I'd grill some

hamburgers.”

“Should I pick up anything?”

“Nope. Got it in hand.” He sighed. “It’s good to be home.”

After dropping Bryson off at his house, Christie completed the rest of the paperwork and scheduled a fundraising email for the following week. She enjoyed being ahead of things. When she left for the day, she felt good with her progress on her endless to-do list. Stopping by her house, she took a quick shower, putting her hair up into a messy bun before shrugging into a shift dress and a pair of flats.

She hoped that seeing the high school yearbook would help them get some ideas on what had happened to Stacy.

~~

“Hello, I’m Christie.”

The woman sported a cute no-nonsense pixie cut, and her eyes sparkled as she smiled at Christie. “Susan. Or my family call me Susie. So use either one.”

Bryson came inside from starting the grill.

"Okay, I've got some kielbasa if anyone wants that, and I'm putting on the burgers now. Either of you want melted cheese on yours?"

"Yes, please." They chimed in unison.

Susie laughed, "In my book, you can't ever have too much cheese."

"Me either. Bryson tells me you used to work at the library."

"Yes, I've transferred over to a university now, but I still enjoy helping students with research. When he told me about you all wanting to do some background research, I said I'd be glad to help. I've already found some news articles from the time we can look at."

"After dinner." Bryson came in carrying a tray of kielbasa and grilled corn on the cob.

"Ooh, that looks yummy. Can I set the table?" Christie asked.

"Sure. That would be great. The burgers should be done pretty quick. I don't have fries, but I bought bags of chips."

"That works for me," said Susie.

"Me too." Christie pulled out plates and

silverware, setting the items down on the table.

After Bryson blessed the food, Christie took a bite of the hamburger. "Oh, this is perfect."

"You're welcome. And that corn is fantastic with the spicy salt, too." He took a bite of the corn, butter dripping onto his plate.

"Bryson tells me you were in Lawton for a while."

"Yes, my mom and uncle live there. I try to visit as much as possible. This time I had another goal in mind, though. There's a job opportunity at the university up there, and I applied. They had me come up for an interview."

"That's exciting. When will you find out if you got the job?"

Susie shrugged. "Hopefully, in the next week or two, but you never know how long the process will take."

"Well, we'll keep our fingers crossed for you." Christie picked up the corn before taking a bite. "Oh, wow. This is like the street corn you get at Fiesta. Really good." She took another bite, savoring the sweet corn, the butter, and the spices.

After they had all eaten their fill, they sat back for a moment, enjoying the meal. Christie was champing at the bit to get started on learning what Suzie had found, but she didn't want to push it either. Finally, Bryson said, "How 'bout we clear off this table so we can see what Susie has discovered?"

Christie hopped up and began clearing away the plates from the table. With the three of them working in tandem, they soon had the dishes washed, and the table cleared. Susie went over and grabbed a messenger bag. "I thought it would be easier to make hard copies of what I'd found." She opened the bag, pulling out a sheaf of paper.

Christie waved toward the stack of papers. "Wow, that's looks like a lot. I'm impressed already."

"The thing with research is that it's always good to go back before the timeframe in question to see if there's anything else that may hold any clues."

"That sounds like a smart idea. I never would

have thought of that. I guess that's why you're the researcher and I'm not!" Christie replied.

"Okay, so here's my process. I took the dates of Stacy's disappearance and worked back a year from then. I wanted to see if I could find anything that spoke about her or the kids she hung around with."

Susie pulled a large book from her bag next. "Because we'll be looking at pictures, it might be good to see faces and equate them to names before we move into the archives."

"That makes sense." Bryson scooted his chair closer to Christie's who sat between them both.

"Okay, I'm not sure what grade levels we're looking for at this point. I know that Stacy was going into her senior year. This is the year when she was a junior." Susie opened the page to a set of freshmen pictures. "Ah, who is that cute kid?"

"Oh, no. Really?" Bryson blushed. In his freshman year picture, he wore a plaid shirt, hair a bit long with a goofy grin on his face.

"Ah, you're so cute. No way. Is that a mullet?" Christie fought back against her laughter.

"Don't start!" He laughed.

They made their way looking at the freshmen pictures, though no one stood out to them, except to Bryson, who traveled a ways down memory lane. "This is fun for me, but not sure why we're not looking at Stacy's classmates."

"There is grade level crossover because of siblings and friendships. You'd be surprised at what you can learn just by doing this backwards."

Susie stopped as Christie pointed toward a picture in the sophomore class. "That's her!"

"Who?"

"I had a young mother come in with her child to see if equine therapy might work for her. She also had her mom with her. I'm pretty sure this is the woman that I met. Though she told me her name was Joy and this says Joyce. She must have shortened her name."

"Oh, I know her. She's like a big online influencer, um, let me think. What is it?" Susie tapped her lips in concentration. "I don't remember, but it'll come to me."

"Wasn't she in your class, Susie?" Bryson

interjected.

"Yes, when she first came, she was dressed more in goth attire. Of course, that didn't go over well at school. She's toned it down in this picture. You know I can remember, she was really bullied—oh no."

"What?" Bryson responded.

Christie answered, "Let me guess. Stacy was one of the bullies."

Susie nodded. "Her and all her cheerleading pals."

Christie stared down into the kohl-rimmed eyes, staring out from the page. "I think we may have found suspect number one."

CHAPTER ELEVEN

After pulling out some paper and making a note of Joyce, the group continued looking through the sophomore class pictures. Bryson noted some people he knew from the time, but few stood out. There were also various older siblings of some of his classmates, but they probably didn't matter. They then turned to the book's junior year section. Besides the individual pictures, they also looked at pictures that had Stacy in group shots. There were some with her cheerleading squad, some with various clubs like the yearbook club or showing her as sweetheart for FFA. In addition, there were other miscellaneous pictures around the school campus.

Christie pointed at a picture. "Look, here's one with her and her boyfriend at the time, Dwight."

Stacy sported a brilliant smile for the camera, while Dwight had his arm slung casually over her shoulder. He wore his football jacket, but as others were looking at the camera, his gaze was focused elsewhere.

Susie bent closer to look. "I wonder what caught his attention?"

"I don't know. But that's a look of longing if I ever saw one," Christie replied.

Susie took a closer look. "Could be. Maybe there was someone else he wanted to date, which is why Stacy was stepping out with the other guy."

"Or maybe it was a cool Charger or truck passing by when they shot the picture." Bryson laughed.

Christie play-punched his arm. "You goof. Well, it could certainly explain his expression. Who are the others in the picture?"

They scanned back through the photos but only found one person. "Maybe they're seniors?"

Sure enough, they found the other boys in the senior class photos. "Looks like they were pretty much all on the football squad. Stacy must have been there when they decided to take a picture of them."

They finished looking through the junior

year. "Okay, I'm going to add her boyfriend to our list. He may not be a suspect at this juncture, but those teenage hormones and all. If someone older had made their move on Stacy and he found out, maybe he went over to confront them and things got out of hand."

"Possibly. But then, wouldn't they have the identity of the other person? Plus, no one else from the school came up as missing when Stacy disappeared," Bryson said.

"Good point. What about her friend on the cheerleading squad? If she had a thing for Dwight or felt Stacy was coming after her boyfriend ... well, there's that old saying about a woman scorned."

Susie interjected. "I think it's good to keep an open mind at this point, neither discounting nor implying any guilt. Currently, it's taking all the data and letting it be placed in front of us. This way, we don't assume anyone had anything to do with the incident."

"Agreed. And good point about collecting all the data. I wonder if any of these people still live here."

Bryson stood and stretched before grabbing the iced tea pitcher and refilling everyone's glasses. "I know her old boyfriend does. He lives out on some property of his family's in a trailer."

"So no football star fame, then?" Christie inquired.

Bryson shook his head. "He had a good future ahead of him, but when Stacy went missing, lots of rumors floated around him. Even though the police ruled him out as a suspect, that didn't stop the gossip mill. Then he ended up getting badly hurt in one of the football games. Some say that the players did it on purpose, but who knows? Anyway, it ended his football scholarship chances."

"Since he still lives here, I think we should go talk to him. Maybe he can give us more insight into what happened that year. What do you think?" Christie wiped the condensation off her tea glass.

"Sure. Not sure if it will help, but I know if I don't go with you, you'll head over there without me."

Christie grinned. "You know me too well. Let's go this weekend. Saturday work?"

He nodded. "Okay. Susie, do you think we've covered everything in the yearbook for now?"

"Yes. How 'bout we take a break, and then we can start up again?"

"Sounds good. Plus, I got the fixin's for hot fudge sundaes."

Christie groaned. "You're killing me."

"Does that mean you don't want one?"

"Are you serious?" She laughed.

He pulled the ice cream from the freezer. "What about you, Susie? You up for ice cream?"

"Absolutely. I'm going to go wash my hands and be back in a minute."

After Susie had left, Bryson hauled Christie over to him, planting a kiss on her. "I've been wanting to do that all night."

"What, your teenage hormones roaring back?"

He grinned. "But for now, I'll settle for lots of hot fudge and whipped cream."

They were putting the finishing touches on the sundaes when Susie returned. They enjoyed the sundaes while Susie inquired more about Christie's work at the rescue. When they had finished their sundaes, they cleared off the table so Susie could share her findings.

"Where did you find all this?" Christie looked at the stack of papers.

"I went to the Patrick Heath Library in Boerne and used their archives. Lucky for us, these years were included." She pulled off the first sheet and laid it in front of the pair.

"As you can see, I went back, first a year, then two. After I didn't find anything else, I moved forward. This is the first mention of Stacy."

Christie gazed at the picture of the attractive young girl, a big smile with teeth full of braces. Behind her stood her parents. They were beaming, and her father had his hand on her shoulder as she held a certificate for some accomplishment. The next one was a picture of a football game, but close to the stands, you could see Stacy with her cheerleading teammates.

"Now, I got to looking at this with a microscope and blew it up." She pulled three sheets of paper out. They were taped together, but unlike the primary picture, these had been highlighted with small arrow stickers and circles.

"Oh, wow. There's her mom and dad." Her mom was talking to a woman sitting beside her. Stacy's father brow was knitted as he frowned. "Who's he looking at?"

"Not sure. I think it's someone that isn't in the picture, but it could be a call on the field."

Next, she pointed out Stacy's boyfriend. He was looking over toward Stacy, who was laughing with her squad.

"Didn't you tell me that the coach was kinda creepy? Maybe he was ogling the girls and Stacy's dad saw it?"

Bryson ran a hand through his hair and sat back in his chair. He crossed his arms over his chest. "Could be. Hard to tell from this angle. Plus, the photographer was focused on the running back, so the other stuff is a bit blurry."

"Well, do you see him with the others?"

Bryson bent forward and scanned the picture. "Nope. Maybe he'd moved down closer to the end zone, which could be closer to the cheerleaders and thus, Stacy's dad's face. If the coach had a reputation, I'm sure the parents would have heard about it, eventually."

"Okay, so we have Stacy, her boyfriend, her parents, possibly the coach. Who do these other arrows point to? They're harder to make out."

Susie produced a magnifying glass. "Here. The others are caught in movement or behind others, but I still wanted to point them out."

Christie took the magnifying glass. Placing it over the specified area, she remarked, "It's Joy or Joyce. Not even sure what to call her. Oh, boy. Looks like she's shooting daggers at Stacy and her friends."

"Well, not surprising if they were bullying her."

Christie sighed. "On one hand, we have this image of an all-American girl and, on the other, a bully."

"Good and bad is within all of us," Bryson

replied.

"Yes, you're right. It just seems wrong somehow. Are you sure that Stacy was part of the bullying?"

"It's what I heard. And we'll never know. Maybe she didn't take part, but not stopping it or going along with it could have been as bad."

"True. Now let me look at these other arrows." She bent over and held the glass over the photo. "It's you!" She handed the magnifier to Bryson.

He looked at the photo. "Oh brother. I look so dorky back then."

"Naw, you were a cutie." Susie winked at her cousin. "All my girlfriends said so."

He blushed at this before stating, "Well, when you got it, you got it."

Christie chuckled, "And humble, too. Well, at least my picture won't be there. I wouldn't have been caught dead at another school's football game."

"Okay, so only one more left. I wasn't sure who this was, so I went back and looked in the yearbook."

Christie and Bryson looked at the girl who was sitting on the bleachers. She wore a letter jacket but wasn't in any uniform. "Who is this?"

"I'm still trying to find out a bit more, but I think she got detention or something. It ended up costing her the head cheerleader position to Stacy."

"That's certainly a motive." Christie set down the magnifying glass. She held up her hand, putting up a finger at a time as she spoke. "Okay, so far, we have the following people we know of that were around Stacy: her parents, the girl she bullied, the one she replaced on the cheer squad, the coach, and her boyfriend. What about ex-boyfriends?"

"That's a good point. If she dumped her last boyfriend for a football guy, that could be another possibility."

"What about his ex-girlfriend? If Stacy stole him away from her, that's another possibility."

Susie sat back. "I'm not sure if I'd be able to find that out with my research, but I could try."

"I think what we need to do is go to a source,"

Christie said.

Bryson shook his head. "I doubt Stacy's dad is up to talking right now."

"No, parents rarely know all the ins and outs of their teen's lives. No. I mean 'the' source. Stacy's boyfriend, Dwight."

CHAPTER TWELVE

They decided to take a break before they got into all the news articles about the time Stacy went missing. They would meet up the following week and go over those reports. In the meantime, Christie and Bryson would go out to Dwight's place and talk to him about what he remembered.

That weekend, Bryson picked up Christie, and they drove out to Dwight's. On the way over, they stopped at the hospital to check in on Stacy's dad, but he'd been released to home care earlier that morning. Dwight lived on his folk's property in a trailer back off the main road. Pulling off onto a dirt track, they bumped along until they saw the trailer in the distance. A couple of dogs ran out from the dilapidated, rusty barn, barking alongside the truck until they got tired and slunk back away to the shade.

While the trailer was old and had seen better days, a shiny Harley sat parked in the front.

"Typical man."

"Not all." Bryson turned toward Christie.

"Well, at least he fits the mold. No wife that you know of?"

"He wasn't in my circle then, and certainly not now." He pulled his truck up to the rickety set of steps and parked. "Let's wait to see if any other mangy mongrels come to greet us before we get out."

As they waited, the door to the trailer opened up. Dwight stood there. His shirt was open, revealing a yellowed and holey tee shirt. He ran his hand through greasy hair and stared at the couple. "if you're coming in, hurry up. I ain't air conditioning the outdoors." He turned and slammed the door behind him.

"Nice fella. And by the looks of him, I'm shocked he's not married," Christie remarked.

"Can't all be as lucky as you are, darling."

She chuckled. After exiting the truck, Bryson took Christie's hand as they made their way up to the door. The simple gesture made Christie feel safe and loved. Dwight had left the door cracked open, but Bryson still knocked on it. From inside, they heard, "Come in. I ain't getting up again."

Christie's nose wrinkled as the smells of tobacco smoke, stale beer, and an overflowing trash can full of fast food wrappers assaulted her senses. Dwight had gone over to a recliner, popping the tab on another beer can as he plopped one foot up on an overturned plastic milk crate. "What can I do you for?"

"We wondered if you'd heard that they determined the body found was that of Stacy Fredrich." Looking around, Christie decided standing was the better option.

"Yeah, I heard. It's a—" He caught himself as he saw Christie staring at him.

Well, at least he still had some manners around women, but that was about as far as it went. He pulled his shirt over his belly, most likely to hide the probable stains of dropped food. His main shirt wasn't any better, as it too had a couple of tears in it, and his jeans were filthy and ragged. Christie waited as he took another sip of his beer.

"I believe you and Stacy were dating back then?"

His gaze went off toward the curtains as if thinking of a response. "Yeah, we hung out."

That was a strange response. She tried another tact. "From what I've heard, people thought you were to blame for her disappearance."

He didn't hold back this time. "That's what they thought all right. But it was a d— lie. They didn't know me, and they didn't know Stacy. She was my best friend. She was the only one I could talk to. She understood." He buried his head in his hand for a minute before rubbing his hand across his scraggly beard. He glanced over at Bryson before looking at Christie.

She continued, "You stayed here instead of going to college?"

"Hurt my arm bad. Got tackled and after that, it was never the same."

"Do you think it was on purpose?"

"Don't know. Don't care."

Christie knew that was a lie, too. By saying that, he'd pretty much said he believed it to be retribution. "So you gave up football, but you never left. Why not?"

"What's the point of going over all this again?"

"Don't you think Stacy deserves justice?"

He stared up at her but said nothing. Gulping down the rest of his beer, he crushed the can in his hand, flinging it toward the overflowing trash bin.

"What about the coach?"

He startled. "What about him? Do you think he may have had something to do with her disappearance? No way. Not him." The vitriol spewed from his mouth.

His eyes met Christie's. And then it all became clear.

"Bryson, I think I dropped my phone, could you go look for it for me?" She hoped he would take the hint.

He hesitated, but she gave a slight nod of her head.

Bryson looked at Dwight, most likely assessing him as a threat before replying, "Okay, but I'll be right outside if you need me."

"We'll be fine." She watched as Bryson walked outside.

"You and Stacy weren't dating, were you?"

He looked at her but said nothing. "Was she covering for you or were you helping her too?"

She could see the fighting going on in his mind, written on his face. Finally, his voice cracked as he spoke. "Let's just say she was helping me, and I was helping her."

"Do you know who she was going out with?"

"Nope. As I said, we were good friends."

"Does anyone know?"

"No!" He pushed up from his chair.

"But you could have told the truth. That alone would have shown your innocence in her disappearance."

"Really? Like I wouldn't have done something in order to get her to keep my secret?"

Christie watched him pace. "But that's so long ago. Things are different now. You don't need to hide."

He paced back and forth. "Don't tell me what I should do. You don't understand anything. I was the big man on campus. I could have had any girl I wanted." He laughed to himself.

"But you didn't."

He shook his head. "I would have been ruined. Then Stacy disappeared. I didn't know if she'd run off with that guy—"

"What guy?"

"She wouldn't tell me. She only said that it would make sense to keep the ruse going and then when I went off to college, it would be normal to break up then. I'd be in a new place and—well, that all came crashing down when they couldn't find her. Fingers started pointing at me as being involved. I couldn't tell them the truth. That would just be a different motive. Then they came at me in practice. I knew it as soon as they started. I felt I deserved it. Maybe I should have done something to make sure Stacy was okay."

He stopped and looked at Christie, his eyes staring into hers.

"See, even now when you know the truth, you still aren't sure I'm innocent. Why would I want to hurt Stacy? She was the only one I could talk to about it." He staggered back over to the recliner, pulling another beer from an ice chest next to the chair. "It don't matter none now."

"Who do you think was the person they found with her?"

"No idea. Could be her boyfriend. Could be someone else." He popped the can open and gulped it down, before wiping his mouth with the back of his hand.

Christie knew she wouldn't get much more out of him. By the amount of beer cans next to his chair and the way his lids were drooping, she knew she was losing him. "Who do you think may have killed her?"

"I wouldn't put it past any of her so-called friends."

"What about Joyce?"

"What about her?"

"I heard she bullied her because she was goth."

He shrugged. "Don't know about that."

"And the coach?"

"Wouldn't put anything past that guy. He was

a piece of work. No one wanted to be around him alone, if you get my drift."

"So he was a—"

"Back in the day, the term was pervert or predator. And he got away with it." He scratched at the recliner's frayed fabric.

So the coach had taken advantage of Dwight. It was disgusting. He would have known that Dwight wouldn't say anything. Had he done the same with Stacy? Or had Stacy threatened to expose the coach for the predator he was? If so, that was a major reason for motive.

"Well, thanks for talking with me. If you think of anything else, call me."

"Yeah, I'll do that," he said sarcastically.

She walked outside to where Bryson had stationed himself near the door. "Did you hear our conversation?"

He nodded. "Do you believe him?"

"That he wouldn't have harmed Stacy? I'm not sure. But it certainly throws a twist in things. Stacy was acting as his girlfriend while all the while she was with someone else. But that means no one else knew who that other person was. So Dwight was helping her hide a secret, too. The question is, did that secret get her killed?" Christie replied before continuing. She folded her arms across her chest. "We need to find out about that coach. The idea of him preying on kids makes me sick to my stomach."

Bryson looked up from his phone. "No need to worry about that. Looks like someone finally had enough."

"Why do you say that?"

"He's serving time in Dilley."

CHAPTER THIRTEEN

After grabbing lunch in town, the pair headed back to Christie's place.

"Hey, can we stop at HEB while we're here? I want to grab a few things."

"Sure. I could use some lunch stuff for this week, too." Bryson pulled into the parking lot and they walked into the store. As he headed over to the deli, Christie made her way toward the canned goods aisle. She had passed one aisle when she spotted Stacy's dad ambling away from her.

"Mister Fredrich!"

He turned toward her, his eyes squinting to see who it was. She strode over to him. "Hi, it's Christie. Christie Taylor. I was there the other day when you had your attack."

"Oh yes, of course. Are you one of the medical team?"

She shook her head. "No, I'd brought over some fried pies for the workers. My friend, Orchid lives there now, so I was checking on the progress.

I heard that you lived there before."

"You heard right. What's that got to do with anything?"

"Well, as you can imagine, my friend Orchid is shaken up about everything's that's happened there."

He didn't respond, so she continued. "She feels a need, maybe more a want, to see justice done for those—"

His voice was raspy as he spoke. "Leave that to the police. They know what they're doing."

"I just figure that we can help if we can find information that may help them. Dwight said—"

"You talked to Dwight?"

She knew she needed to tread carefully here. "Yes. From what he alluded to, it may have been that they were breaking up. That could account for the other person found with Stacy."

Mister Fredrich grabbed at the nearby shelving.

"Are you okay, Mr. Fredrich? Do you need to sit down?"

"Naw. It's just this medication they've got me

on now. Makes me a bit woozy sometimes."

"You probably don't need to be out and about on your own. Or at least use one of those scooters."

He shooed at her like an annoying fly. "I don't like being cooped up in that house all day. And I can take care of myself."

Christie suppressed a smile, as he sounded just like her Pop when he had any of his personal freedom taken from him. "Well, how about I help you by at least carrying your basket or getting you a cart that you can hold on to?"

He took a deep breath. "A cart might be good."

Just at that moment, Bryson came down the aisle, joining them. "Would you please grab a basket for Mister Fredrich? He's a bit woozy and a cart may be good to carry his stuff."

"Certainly. You want me to grab one for you, too?"

"Probably wouldn't hurt. Thanks."

He nodded and headed back up the aisle to go find a basket for them.

"Mister Fredrich, I truly don't want to cause you more pain. I'd just like to help you get closure and justice for your daughter. Have they let you know who the other person is yet?"

He shook his head. Staring up at Christie, she saw the pain in his eyes. "Have you ever lost someone close to you? Because there is no closure. There's only grief. As for justice, it's coming. I know it. I feel it. As the saying goes, 'Vengeance is mine. I will repay, says the Lord.' No one outruns God."

Christie remained silent. It was clear the man had suffered loss. First, his daughter. Then his wife. And now his health. Bryson returned with a larger and smaller cart. After transferring Mister Fredrich's items to the larger basket, they watched as he shuffled down the aisle.

"What did you say?"

"How do you know I said anything?"

He cocked his head and looked at her with an expression of disbelief.

"Okay, I said that we'd talked to Dwight. He didn't—or doesn't—know about the truth of him and Stacy. As far as he's letting on, they were still a couple. And they still haven't said anything about the second person they found. I think that person is the real key to whatever happened that night."

"Okay, well, here's a thought. It's none of our business. I'm not even sure why I agreed to let Suzie do all that work for us."

"Because people deserve justice. I don't think Orchid will ever move back there if there's no resolution over everything."

"Where is Orchid now?"

"As far as I know, she's still down at the coast with her sister. Speaking of relatives, can we meet with Suzie to go over the information she found after the disappearance? I mean, she's already done the work. We owe it to her to look at everything."

Bryson added a few jars of salsa to the basket. "Fine. Do you want to do it at my house again?"

"Let's do it at my place. I can do something easy for dinner, like King Ranch Casserole and a salad. Which means we need to go back so I can grab the stuff I'll need."

After checking out, they walked with the basket out to the truck. Bryson hauled the bags into the space behind the club cab. "So much for picking up a few items."

"I know. It never fails that I end up thinking of more things when I get in there." She hopped up into the truck as Bryson shut the door, walking around the other side. He started up the truck, and they enjoyed listening to music on the radio.

"Did you like high school?" Christie asked.

"Not particularly. It was just a part of life. You?"

"Same. I think I lived more in the moment then. It seemed like a simpler time. I can't imagine the things kids nowadays face, along with all the social and regular media bombardment."

"Yes, I'm glad we grew up without all that. We sound like those old folks—in my day—" He mimicked.

They laughed.

"I walked to school 1800 miles, and both ways were uphill." Christie chimed in before growing serious. "You know we can look back and laugh, but Stacy and this other person never got the chance to live. It's heartbreaking."

"You're right. I need to be better about being grateful for each day."

"Me too. And for those I love. I'm grateful for you, Bryson."

His face lit up. "Back at ya."

They arrived at Christie's to find Lana sitting on the steps up to Christie's cob house.

"Hey you. Did I forget we were going to meet?"

Lana shook her head. "Naw. I knew you wouldn't be here."

Christie's face bore a puzzled look.

"I brought you a present." Lana stood up from the steps, wiping her hands on her jeans.

"A present?"

Lana nodded. "Follow me." The pair followed Lana to the back of the house, where a large trampoline stood.

"What's this?"

Lana gestured toward it. "It's a trampoline!"

"I can see that. I mean, um, why?"

"You said you wanted to get a rebounder. Well, this is even better. It doesn't have the sides up yet, but I had them put it as close to the house as possible for now. Once you decide where you want it, then we'll move it there."

"I don't know what to say."

"Thank you would be good." Lana beamed.

Christie knew that a trampoline was a lot different from a small rebounder she could keep in her office, but she didn't want to hurt Lana's feelings. "Thanks. I appreciate you thinking of me."

"You're welcome." Lana came over and hugged Christie. "Ready to try it out?"

"We've got groceries in the truck that need to get in the house."

Bryson interjected. "I can take them up. Go ahead."

Before long, Christie and Lana were jumping and laughing. Bryson came back to where they were at. "I've got to go, someone's electricity has an issue. I'll see you later."

"Sounds good." Christie bent over and placed her hands on her knees. Jumping really got the heart rate going. "I can see how this would be good for working off steam and getting the blood pumping. I think I'm going to like this. What made you think of it?"

"I don't know. It was strange, really. A person came in, and they said they were getting rid of it and wondered if we could use it. And then it just came to me. 'Give it to Christie.' So that's what I did."

"I appreciate it, but it probably would have worked well for some of our therapy clients."

"Yes, I thought so too. But you know what they say—always say to listen to that inner voice. I figure if you end up not using it, we can always move it over there."

"Good point. Maybe even inside a barn in the winter. Okay, let's get off here and go grab a drink. Soda or iced tea?"

"Trying to be good, so I'll stick with the iced tea."

"Me too."

Upstairs, Christie pulled the pitcher from the fridge, pouring them each a glass of unsweetened iced tea. They sat down, enjoying the moment. "Thanks for being such a good friend and thinking of me. I never would have thought about getting a trampoline, but it was really fun to get out there and just bounce up and down. It's like it gets rid of any worries."

"Are you worried about something?"

"We've been trying to figure out who may have wanted Stacy out of the picture." She caught Lana up to speed with the recent conversation with Dwight.

"Hmm, not sure what to think about that. In one way, it seems you should let him off the hook, and in another way—"

"Motive for murder."

CHAPTER FOURTEEN

Christie had placed the casserole in the oven when she heard Bryson's truck pull up. He bounded up the stairs, carrying a bouquet of yellow roses. She greeted him at the door with a kiss.

"What's all this?"

"Yellow roses for my yellow rose of Texas." He kissed her forehead as she buried her face in the flowers.

"These actually have a fragrance."

"Yes, I think they're called Fragrant Perfume or something like that."

"No matter. I call them lovely. Thank you." She walked over to the kitchen where she pulled down a large clear vase. After prepping the roses, she set them on the table.

"Need help with anything?" Bryson said.

"No. I decided to make a build-your-own salad, so everything's laid out for that." She heard Suzie's car had arrived. "Perfect timing. The casserole will be about twenty more minutes, so that will give us time to review what she found."

Bryson opened the door, and Suzie stepped inside. She had the big messenger bag over her shoulder and was carrying a covered plate. "I didn't know if you had dessert figured out, but I brought Hepburn brownies."

"Hepburn brownies?"

"Yes, supposedly these are, I mean, were Katharine Hepburn's favorite brownies."

Christie peeked under the cover. "Who doesn't love brownies? They look delicious. Thanks for bringing them."

Once the trio settled around the table, Suzie brought out the next batch of paperwork. She undid the large clip holding the first batch. "I did the various articles by date. I figured that would help with the timeline."

"Makes sense." Christie scooted her chair forward to look at the first article. The headline read Local Girl Missing. "I thought they were first treating it as a runaway."

"They did, but you can see this is a day or two after she was reported as not coming home. And back then they didn't have Amber alerts like we do now."

"Oh, that's right. When did that start again? I think around 1996 or so. Here's another sad fact. Did you know that Texas has the most alerts of all the states?"

"No. I didn't know that. Well, in any case, we'll never know the circumstances around Stacy's disappearance. I found out that her dad moved out to the new house, but the mom stayed in the smaller house. So Stacy had been living there at the time of her disappearance." She read the article. "So it sounds like they didn't get concerned until the following morning or afternoon. It says here that she often stayed with friends after football games."

"But wouldn't they have wondered about her the next morning?"

"I doubt it. If she was anything like me back then, I caught up on my sleep on Saturdays. So they probably wouldn't have even thought of checking on her until the afternoon. And of course, no cell phones back then either. So it would have been calling her friend's houses."

"Good point. Yet doesn't it seem weird that they didn't search around her own house? I mean, she was discovered at the house."

"Sadly, it doesn't seem like they searched the area where the concrete was going to be laid. I think they still thought of it as a runaway at that point. Plus, look at this."

Susie pulled a piece of paper from another stack.

Christie looked at it. "Her father sat on the city's board. Wouldn't that have meant they even did more to find her?"

"Who knows. That's one thing where we'll probably will never get an answer."

Bryson flipped through to the other articles. "Most of these look the same. Description, etc. Parents asking for Stacy to call them or for any information."

Christie looked over Bryson's shoulder at the picture of the parents taken outside of their home. Their faces raw with grief. Others stood around them. "These must be Stacy's friends. Do we know their names?"

Suzie pulled the yearbook out of her pack. The trio went through the individual pictures, looking for faces.

"Hold on. I don't want to write on the photo, so let me get some paper to make notes." She got up and grabbed a notepad, drawing stick figures to mimic the figures in the picture.

"Okay, who's that?" She pointed out a girl whose eyes were puffy from crying.

"Let's see." Bryson moved his finger down the page in the yearbook. "No one here." He did the same thing on the next page. Finally, when he'd turned the page, the girl's photo appeared.

"Here she is." He pointed at the young woman smiling for the camera. Donna.

"Wait, I think that was Stacy's best friend. I wonder where she is now." Christie picked up her phone and typed in her name. "If she's married, it's going to be more difficult with a different last name, but ya never know."

A bunch of pictures popped up. Some of them older shots, but one grabbed Christie's attention.

"Oh, look. She either kept her maiden name or uses if for business."

"What does she do?"

"Owns an interior design firm in San Antonio. D's Designs. That could be why she kept the last name, or she started it before she got married, but kept the company name. Hmm, I wonder how we could talk to her. I guess I'll have to go over and check out her shop."

"You could just call?"

"People have a harder time hanging up on you in person. Plus, the expressions on people's faces relay half of the communication. You up for a jaunt to a design showroom?"

Bryson shook his head. "That's a no from me. I bet Lana would go with you, though."

"Okay, I'll ask her." She set her phone down as the oven timer dinged. "Food's ready. Let's take a break from this for a while."

After moving the paperwork to the sofa, Bryson wiped down the table while Christie pulled the bubbling King Ranch casserole from the oven.

"That smells delicious." Suzie said.

"I hope you like it. I kept it a bit more mild than usual in case you didn't like heat in your food."

"Thanks. I love it but my body doesn't. What are the main ingredients? Believe it or not, I've always heard of it, but never had it before." She took the silverware Bryson handed her.

"Really? I think of it as a Texas staple in some respects. But maybe not. Anyway, it's basically what I'd call a Texan lasagna. You combine one can each of cream of chicken and mushroom soup along with a can of tomatoes with chiles. I often add another can of just chiles as I like it a bit spicier. Then add the chicken broth to make a sauce. From there you add a bit of the sauce, then cut up corn tortillas, shredded chicken, more sauce, and cheese. Then repeat. I added onions too, but I left those out this time. I have chopped onion, black olives, cilantro, sour cream, and some salsa, if you want to add it to yours. I also have avocado I sliced for the salad."

"Do you add any spices to it?"

"You can add your favorite spices. I normally

just do onion and garlic powder along with a bit of cumin. Sometimes if I'm making it just for me, I'll also add coriander as well. You can also add in some of the sour cream if the sauce mixture gets too diluted. It makes a really nice creamy sauce.

"Sounds good. Can't wait to try it." Suzie took a seat and Christie set the hot dish on a trivet Bryson had set on the table.

They took a break from what they'd been discussing before, focusing on some of the things they recalled from their youth. The food was good and the laughter contagious. They had all started on second helpings when a knock at the door startled them.

CHAPTER FIFTEEN

Christie went over to the door to find Pop there.

"Pop, I didn't hear your truck."

He chuckled. "It's probably that music you've got cranked up."

"You want to join us? I made King Ranch casserole." She pointed at the casserole dish.

"That sounds mighty good. But I already ate."

"How 'bout this? If there's any left, I'll bring you some over tomorrow."

"Okay." He replied.

"Now, what are you doing here? I've told you I'm not crazy about you going up and down my stairs, especially at night."

"I was coming back home, and when I turned in the lane, there was a woman sitting outside in her car. She was staring toward your house."

Bryson said, "That's not creepy at all."

"Who was it?" Christie asked.

"No one I know. When I drove up, she rolled down her window and said she'd taken a wrong turn and had pulled off to check her GPS."

"That makes sense. I've done that sometimes." Susie replied.

Christie joined Pop out on the deck and glanced out toward the road. There was silence, and they were far enough back that all she saw was darkness. "And then what happened?"

"She turned around and drove off."

Bryson rose from his chair and walked over to Christie. "I don't like the sound of that. Y'all should let me put up a light out there or put in a gate."

"Nah, I've lived here forever without either." Pop hit his hat against his thigh, knocking off the dust.

"I'm sure Pop's right. It was just some person who got lost." She beckoned her father inside. She glanced back toward the road, and as she did, a shiver went up her spine.

~~

After Pop went home, and they'd worked through the rest of the articles, the group called it a night. After getting permission from Suzie to keep the articles for a bit, she bid them goodnight. She shut off the lights, locking the doors before glancing at the time. It was later, but she knew Pop liked to get a text from her to let him know all was well. Even though she'd seen him just a few hours before, she texted him to find out he'd made it home okay. It had become a habit for Christie too, since their houses were far enough away that she might not know if anything had happened to her father.

She sent off a text.

Night, Pop. Love you.

Love you too, girlie. Sweet dreams.

You too.

Even though she'd never had children of her own, Christie could imagine wanting to ensure your child was safe. She was thankful for Pop, and when she'd decided to move back home to Comfort, he'd been thrilled. Now that the constant requests from developers to buy their property had died down, life was getting into an easier flow.

She curled up in bed before grabbing her ereader. She needed something light to take her thoughts off the tragedy that had surrounded them the last few days. She also needed to call Orchid to see how she was doing. Though she figured that she or her sister would have called if they needed anything. She flipped open the reader to continue reading. The story by author Melissa Storm revolved around second chances at romance and chihuahua puppies.

It wasn't long before her eyelids were growing heavy, and she set aside the book for the night. She had a busy schedule for the next few days. Then she'd get Lana to go with her into San Antonio to speak with Stacy's high school friend.

As she drifted to sleep, her mind wouldn't settle. She felt that the key to understanding the deaths all led back to why they were killed. Once the motive was clear, the means and opportunity often fell into place. It was that *why* that had to be addressed first. Maybe she'd get more answers from Stacy's old high school friend.

~~

Lana and Christie made sure that the rescue

was in capable hands before heading down into San Antonio. Lana was excited as she loved attending the Parade of Homes and other design events, so she was ready to visit the showroom. They stopped for a bite to eat before heading to the design studio located off 281.

"Okay, so let's get our stories straight. I'm your friend, and you're looking at possibly doing some new window treatments."

Lana laughed. "That's not much of a story. It's the truth."

"Yeah, well, they always say to stick to the truth as much as possible. However, you aren't wanting to pay thirty to fifty thousand to kit your house out in upholstered valances and drapes."

"Oh, my word. Really?"

"Yes, really. And it's probably even more now. That was from a designer I knew back years ago."

"Geez. I wonder if we should have dressed up before we came."

"We look fine." Christie smoothed her skirt.

"Okay, well, it's go time." They pulled up to the building with D's Designs on the signage above the door. She glanced over at Christie. "I still think we should have tried out secret service outfits again." She winked.

Lana and Christie had pretended to go undercover to gain information before. She hoped that they wouldn't find what they'd found last time, which was a dead body.

They walked into the front door, and a lady with bright red lipstick and lacquered nails to match held up one finger. She finished a conversation she was having on the phone before moving over toward them. "Good morning, ladies. I'm Jill. What can I help you with?"

"We wanted to look around. I'm building a house outside of Boerne and wanted to see what my options might be," Lana responded.

They'd agreed that sticking as close to the truth as possible would be the best way forward. And Lana said it wasn't a lie, simply acting. Christie considered that more semantics than truth, but she went along with Lana's playacting.

"I'd be happy to show you around."

Lana replied, "I was told to ask for Donna. Is

she in?"

The woman gave a tight smile. "I'll have to see. Do you have an appointment with her?"

"We promise not to take too long. Or maybe we should come back. We're checking out a few firms," Lana said.

Christie struggled to hold back a chuckle. She had to give it to Lana, she knew the right things to say. No wonder they had recently scored a better deal on some horse medications.

"Please, feel free to have a look around. I'll see if Donna's available."

Christie noted the woman sizing them up, but she had no worries about that when Lana raised her arm to look at her Cartier watch. She also had a rock on her finger that Christie hadn't noticed before. Where had Lana gotten these?

"We'll look around but can't take too much time. I have an appointment with the builder—"

The woman's face lit up, and she asked, "Oh, who's your builder? We work with many of the premier builders here."

Christie jumped in. "I doubt you'd know him.

She just moved here and asked her architect to do her house here. I think that's what you mean, isn't it?" She faced Lana.

"Yes, so much on my mind lately, as you can imagine."

"Of course. If you'd like to go over to the adjoining room, we keep some gallery photos of our work there along with some fabrics and other samples."

"That would be wonderful." They moved toward the other room as Jill went to hunt Donna down.

"Whew, I'm glad you had a comeback. I didn't think about it."

"It's fine. Now, on to Plan B. I'll just have to wait for the right timing and hope it seems sincere."

Lana went over and ran her hands over a sample of fabric. "This is wonderful."

They were startled by a voice behind them. "It has a nice hand to it, doesn't it? I can see you have good taste in fabrics." Donna approached them, her sky high heels clicking on the floor. She wore a tailored jumpsuit that fit her perfectly. Her hair was cut in the latest style, and she wore minimal though impressive makeup. "I'm Donna." She held out her French-tipped manicured hand, which Lana took.

Classic. That was the word that came to Christie. It probably went over well with her old-money clientele.

"I'm Lana and this is my friend, Christie."

She turned toward Christie. This was Christie's moment. "I'm sorry, have we met before?"

The woman's face tightened as she sought to place Christie. "I'm not sure. I'm sorry. Did we meet at the club?"

Christie had no idea which club, so she simply shrugged and replied. "I just feel like I've seen you before. Could be that you remind me of someone."

The woman laughed. "I have that happen sometimes, too. Now, Jill said that you had asked for me. Were you referred from one of my clients?"

Lana had already told Christie what she'd

planned to say if this came up. "No, to be honest, that was a fib. But I enjoy meeting the owner. It tells me a lot about the establishment, and I've seen and love your work—" She waved toward the gallery of Parade of Homes interiors.

Again, another true statement from Lana.

"Oh, thank you. They're a lot of work, but it's a great way to showcase up and coming new design ideas. Now, what can I help you with today?"

Lana played the role perfectly of a well-to-do woman who was looking into various furnishings and window treatments. It wasn't surprising she could pull it off as well as she did, but they had enough wealthy donors and she had plenty of role models to choose from to emulate.

It wasn't long though before she caught Christie's eye and mouthed 'get on with it.'

Christie nodded and then exclaimed. "I know, high school! Weren't you on the cheerleading team for Boerne?"

Donna looked over at Christie, a surprised look on her face. "Yes, though it's been a long time since then. What made you think of that?"

"I think it was that they discovered Stacy Fredrich's body. Did you hear about that?"

"Wait, what?" The shocked expression looked real.

"Oh, I'm sorry. I thought you'd probably seen it on the news."

"I've been out of state at a trade event in California. When was this announced?"

Christie felt sorry for the woman. The shock and pain on her face looked real, or she was a good actress. "Can we sit down?" She pointed over to a large conference table with chairs around it.

Donna nodded and sat at the table, her hands cradling her forehead. "I thought she'd—"

"What?" Lana inquired.

Donna shook her head. "It's a long time ago."

"So you thought she'd run away?"

"No, not run away. Well, I guess technically, yes. She was going to leave with—" She stopped.

Christie knew if they didn't keep her talking, she'd probably dismiss them. "I heard you were good friends. So you thought she was going to leave with Dwight?"

"Him? No. She'd fallen for someone else. Someone her father wouldn't approve of. They'd kept it secret. I can't believe it. All this time." Donna said.

Lana spoke to Christie, "That could explain the second body."

"What?" Donna bolted from her chair.

"They found two bodies. They've identified Stacy's but so far haven't released anything about the second person. Do you have any idea who might have wanted Stacy out of the picture or—"

Donna's brows knitted together. "Who are you really?"

Christie decided to come clean. "Our friend, Orchid, lives in the house where they found them."

"In a house. Where?"

"Actually, in the backyard. She was found under a gazebo."

Donna cried out. "Oh, no. That's what her parents put up in the backyard because Stacy had always said that she wanted one."

"When did they do that?"

"It was some months after Stacy was gone. I think they realized she wasn't coming back. They'd already poured a slab for a storage shed but changed it to a gazebo."

Lana glanced over at Christie, knowing this could be the end of their conversation. "I believe you, and Stacy had a bit of a competition going between you. She ended up taking the head role after something happened and you had to sit out games."

Donna's face clouded over. "You think I had something to do with this? You have a nerve coming in here, pretending to want design help. You need to leave now!"

Jill rushed into the room, looking at the group. "What's going on?"

"They are leaving. Please escort them out."

"We're sorry. We didn't mean to cause—" Lana stopped as she saw the fury in Donna's gaze.

They headed toward the entrance, but it was Christie who picked up on Donna, muttering under her breath, "She finally did it."

CHAPTER SIXTEEN

They drove back to the rescue as Lana had left her vehicle there earlier. She wanted to check in and make sure everything went well during the day with the new vet interns. Since she was already there, Christie popped into the main office. There were a few messages on her desk during the time she was out. One was from the young mother who had decided to put her daughter into the therapy program. Christie's thoughts went back to the mother. She hoped she'd be able to talk with her if she joined them next time, too. It might also give her the opportunity to speak with Joyce, Joy. She had to remember that she'd shortened her name. As she thought of the name, she was reminded of someone who brought her joy.

Since she had a moment, she picked up her phone and called Orchid. She answered with a much bubblier voice than the last time Christie had spoken with her.

"Hello, Christie. So good to hear from you."

"Hi, Orchid. Are you still down at the coast?"

"Just for today. Then we'll be heading home. I have to face the house at some point, and I've been told that I can return." She sighed.

"Sorry, you're having to deal with this, Orchid. When you get back into town, let me know, and I'll treat you all to dinner."

"You're so sweet and no need to do that, but it would be nice to see you. Any updates on the case?"

Orchid knew Christie well enough to know that she couldn't sit back and not try to help solve a mystery. "A few things. I'd be happy to share with you. We've been able to chat in person with a few people on the possible list of suspects, but still have some more to go through. Bryson's cousin, Suzie has helped a lot with pulling information from the past."

"That sounds wonderful. Well, give my love to all, and I'll see you tomorrow. Then we can connect on where and when to meet for dinner."

"Has your sister been on the Riverwalk yet?"

"No. Are you thinking about going down

there?"

Christie replied. "We could do the tourist boat ride and eat some good 'ol Tex-Mex. Do you think she'd like that?"

"Certainly. I always enjoy the boat ride too, even though I've done it a few times in the past. She's calling me so talk tomorrow. Bye." Orchid rung off.

Christie set her phone down on her desk before picking it up again. She hit the number for Bryson.

It rang a few times before he answered. "Hiya."

"Hi. Sorry if I'm bothering you."

"You are never bothering me. I always love when I see your name on my phone screen."

She heard beeping with him getting into his truck. "Is this a good time to talk?"

"Sure. I just wanted to get inside my truck and turn on the AC. It's a scorcher out there today."

"As opposed to every other day?"

His laugh was deep and masculine. "You got me there. Now what's on your mind, pretty lady?"

"I thought I might go through the articles Suzie gave us one more time tonight. You up for that?"

"Certainly. You want me to pick up some BBQ on the way over?"

"That would be great. I'm thinking you could give the male perspective on everything that's been going on. So far, we talked to Dwight, and today, Lana and I chatted with Stacy's girlfriend and cheer teammate, Donna Dixon."

"How'd that go?"

"Not great. She'd been out of town and hadn't heard about them finding Stacy. She got angry, thinking we were accusing her of being involved. But I think she knows more than she said today."

"Hmm, understandable, I guess. So, who else is in your crosshairs?"

"I want to look more into that creepy coach. I keep thinking that it would need to be someone really strong to kill two people."

"Not necessarily. Especially if one was killed before the other one."

"That's an interesting premise. So you're

saying, one person was killed and then days or weeks or even months later, the other person was killed?"

"It wouldn't have to be even that long. Listen, my guys are calling me. We're pulling wire, so I need to go help them. See you around six thirty?"

"That works great. See you then." She hesitated for a split second before stating, "Love you."

"Love you too."

After being on her own and an independent woman for much of her life, it felt a bit strange to have found love now. All she knew was that Bryson had been a godsend, and she was happy that she would be spending the rest of her life with him. Pop had made no secret that he was happy that she had Bryson as he would talk about, not knowing how much longer he'd be around. She hated him talking like that, even if she knew it to be true. If anything, Pop would probably outlive them all simply because of his orneriness.

She typed up a few email responses and then made her way out toward her truck. She had almost gotten in when she saw Lana wave at her from the other barn. Christie walked over to her. "We missed it, but earlier today they put out a forensic sketch of the second person. They said it's a young male, possibly Hispanic ethnicity."

"Interesting. So this could be the secret that Stacy was hiding from her father if he had an issue with her dating him."

"I don't know that much about that. Maybe we could try to talk to Donna or one of Stacy's other friends about it."

"Yeah, I think I'll pass on Donna. That didn't end well at all."

Lana scratched her arm. "Ugh. Must have gotten a mosquito bite. Also, they noted that they were having a celebration of life service for Stacy, but it was going to be family and close friends only."

"I wonder where they're having it at."

Lana shrugged. "Not sure, but I can understand them not wanting it to be a media circus."

"So Stacy's mom is going to come back from

Florida?"

"Probably. She may already be here now as I thought it showed her and Stacy's dad standing off to the side when they had the announcement."

"Hmm. Well, once we have a name for the second victim, that could help with motive for sure. I don't know if this helps or causes more pain for Stacy's folks."

"I'll see if I can find a link to the announcement and email it to you."

"That would be great. You heading home?"

Lana shook her head. "I'm going to change out of these clothes and stay close to this mare tonight. The kids are at home, and Curtis is over with them, so I don't feel I need to rush home."

"Okay, well, if you need me, you know where to find me." Christie waved before getting up into the truck. The drive home was easy, and she looked at the clock. She had some time before Bryson would arrive, so she could get some chores done out at the barn. After changing into a pair of shorts and a tank top, she made her way down the steps, glimpsing the trampoline off at the back.

She should probably move it away from the house. Maybe when Bryson came over, they could lift it and pull it by themselves.

Entering the barn, she was grateful for its dim interior, that had kept it cooler than the outdoor temps. She refilled the interior water tanks and checked the feed. Everything looked good, so she wouldn't have to get all sweaty and take another shower. She checked on the horses and then went back up to her house. It was too hot to sit outside, so she went in and pulled the articles off the table.

Sitting on the couch, she went through the pictures. In many of the older shots, it was evident that both parents were highly involved in Stacy's life. They were often seen in the background of games or other events, both wearing the smiles of proud parents. Christie wondered why they'd never had more than one child. It certainly looked as if they were heavily engaged in Stacy's life. Had it been by choice or because they couldn't have any other children? She jotted a note down on a pad she had brought over to the couch with her.

She also thought back to what Bryson had

said earlier. Had the two young people been killed at the same time or individually? And if so, why?

CHAPTER SEVENTEEN

By the time Bryson arrived, Christie had filled a page with ideas and questions. Though a lot more questions than answers. He came in the unlocked front door, carrying bags of delicious smelling food. They sat down and enjoyed chopped brisket sandwiches, potato salad and coleslaw. He'd also gotten them banana pudding for dessert.

"More tea?" Christie held up the pitcher as he licked some BBQ sauce from his fingers. He nodded.

She poured the tea over the ice cubes, adding more to her own glass. She sighed and sat back in her chair. "That was yummy. Hit the spot. Thanks."

"You're welcome. I'd driven by it on the way to the job, so I had it on my mind." He took another bite of his brisket.

"They put out a facial reconstruction today of the second victim. Did you hear about that?"

He nodded, chewing. Finally, he wiped his

mouth with a napkin before speaking. "One of the guys had heard about it. I haven't seen it yet. Have you?"

"No. Lana was going to send it over to me, but not sure when she'll get to it as she's hanging out with a pregnant mare. You know Stacy was an only child. I've been wondering if that was on purpose or they simply couldn't have other children."

"Not sure and don't know how we'd find out. We certainly can't ask."

"We may try to speak to Donna again, as she could give us some insights on it."

"Why do you think that matters?"

Christie shrugged. "I don't know, to be honest. It's just one more question on my endless list of questions. I feel like if we can get rid of the easy questions with answers, it can help us focus on the answers we really need."

"Possibly." He sighed and rubbed his belly. "I think I may have enjoyed that a little too much."

She laughed. "Well, don't blame me. I didn't force you to eat that second half."

"I know that I'll have to wait on the pudding for now."

Christie rose. "Good idea. Let me put them in the fridge, and we can look over the articles again and see if anything stands out."

After placing the pudding in the fridge, Christie topped off their iced teas before wiping the table clean. She then brought over the pages Suzie had copied.

"Okay, here's what we know. If I miss anything, you jump in."

"Okie dokie."

"Stacy was dating Dwight. However, from our recent meeting, they were both helping each other out by pretending to date each other. Ooh—that means he must know who Stacy was dating. We need to speak with him again."

She looked at a notepad where she'd added some suspect names. "Okay, next up is her friend, Donna. She may have also known about the pretense between Stacy and Dwight. Or maybe not. From what I've gathered, it seems they could have been frenemies. I'd really like to talk with her again, but I'm not holding my breath on that one."

Bryson slumped back in his chair, crossing his legs and arms across his chest. "But would she have had the means or the opportunity to kill two people?"

"Good question. You want to move over to the sofa so you can stretch out? I know you've had a long day."

He nodded. "That would be great." As Christie picked up the items, he took their teas, setting one next to a chair. He pulled off his work boots, putting his feet up on the couch. "Oh, yes, that's much better. Continue."

"Okay, then we have the creepy coach. From our talk with Dwight, it sounds like he could definitely have been involved. I wonder if we can find out anything about what happened to him."

Bryson pulled his phone from his shirt pocket. "Let me call Suzie and see what she thinks."

Christie waited as he connected with Suzie, letting her know about this new direction. "Okay, great. Thanks." He disconnected the call. "She said she'd get back to us."

"We need to do something nice for her. She's been a huge help."

He nodded. "Agreed. What, or should I say, who next?"

"There's the person they bullied. Though why go after the second person? I think it's a long shot, but it would still be good to chat with her and see what she remembers from that time."

"It could be that Stacy was the main target. Think about it. It was her house. It would have been a lot easier to attack the other person elsewhere."

"Good point." She opened to a new page and wrote Questions along the top. Who was the intended victim? Why at Stacy's house?

She continued writing some notes when she heard soft snoring. She smiled at the sleeping Bryson. Of course, he was worn out from his job that started early, yet he didn't hesitate when she asked him to go over everything again. She pulled her feet up under her and worked her way through the articles again, letting him sleep.

So far, they have four primary suspects. The pretense boyfriend, her frenemy, the creepy coach, and the bullied teen. Others around her at the time included her parents, and who else? Certainly, there would be teachers or other teens that weren't even in the mix. Though that went back to another aspect. The boy who was found with her. Maybe he was the intended victim, and she had been the one to get caught up in it. For instance, if another boy had wanted to go out with Stacy, this guy would have gotten in the way. But you don't kill someone for that. Though in the last years, crazy stories of such things had made headlines. She sighed. She really wanted to put Orchid's mind at ease. The more she thought about it, the more she needed to talk with Orchid about when she moved into the house. It made sense that Stacy's mom had finally decided that Stacy wasn't coming back and wanted a fresh start in Florida.

It would be interesting to speak to Stacy's mom, as she might supply some insights too. She was sure that Stacy's parents would be grateful for any help they could give to solve this mystery. She'd have to see if Orchid was in touch with the woman when they met.

Christie turned to another sheet of paper marking up four boxes on the page. In one, she put Stacy's name. In the other one, she wrote Louis. For some reason, it felt better to write a name, even if it wasn't his real one.

Under that, she listed the various people around Stacy. If Louis knew Stacy, how many of the others on the list did he also know? It would be so helpful if they could match up those from both sides. For now, she left the area under his name blank.

Bryson's phone rang, jolting him from sleep. He rubbed his hand over his face before grabbing at the phone. "Hello?"

Christie watched as he listened, nodding his head. When he finished listening, he ended it by saying, "We owe you, Suz. Talk soon. Bye."

He hung up the phone, rubbing his hands across his eyes and letting out a big yawn. "Sorry 'bout that. The heat just takes it out of me."

"If anyone needs to apologize, it should be me. This could have waited until the weekend. So what did she say?"

"She's something. I can't believe she found out so much information on the coach in such a short time."

Great. So?"

"Well, she'll give us more of it, but bottom line, I did some digging on what he's serving time for in Dilley."

"Okay. For?"

"Assault and murder."

CHAPTER EIGHTEEN

After sending Bryson home for the evening, Christie cleaned up and went to bed. But sleep wouldn't come as she tossed and turned. Could it be that simple? If the coach had felt Stacy would expose him, he could have come after her or them. But it might also mean a dead end for them finding out the truth of what happened. Doubtful he would admit to the crime even if he'd done it. Exhausted at getting nowhere, she finally fell asleep.

The following day, the lack of sound sleep had affected her mood, so she stayed in her office much of the morning. She would be meeting with Orchid for dinner, but they'd chatted that morning as Orchid planned to go home and get some clothing. When asked if Christie could join her, she'd noted that she could slip away from the nonprofit later in the afternoon. The day drug by, and she was glad when it finally was close enough for her to leave. She finished saving the spreadsheet she'd been working on and shut down her computer. Calling over to the vet barn, she spoke with Lana, letting her know that she was taking off a bit early to meet Orchid.

A thought came to her, and she decided to call Dwight to get his feedback about the coach. The phone rang a few times before Dwight came on the line, his words slurred. He must already be deep in the booze. "H..ello?"

"Dwight, this is Christie. I wondered if you knew that Coach Bundy was arrested some years ago for assault and murder?"

"I'd heard some rumors, but what's it to me?"

"I was only wondering how it had affected you and—"

He interrupted. "No skin off my nose. But he probably deserves where he is."

"Do you think he had anything to do with Stacy's death?"

"How should I know? I'm not, or I wasn't her keeper."

Christie fought against her temper but ended up lashing out at him. "But you said you were her friend? Don't you care what happened to her? You should have told the truth about your relationship."

Silence.

Oh, no. She had gone too far.

He hissed through the line. "You don't tell me what I should or shouldn't do. And if you say anything, you're going to be sorry."

"Are you threatening me?"

"I'm saying that you best keep your gab shut about me and Stacy. She was my pal then. But I can't help her now."

Christie tried another tact. "Do you know who it was she was dating?"

"No. She just told me it was no one I knew and that her dad would have a fit if he found out. And that's..."

"Hello? Are you there?"

Snoring came through the phone into her ear. Christie ended the call. What a waste of a life. Maybe she could find someone to talk to him about his drinking. She stood and put the phone in her purse. Grabbing her keys, she headed to her truck and over to Orchid's.

On arriving at the house, she noticed two vehicles parked out front. One looked familiar. Then she remembered. It was Stacy's dad. After exiting the truck, she heard raised voices in the back. Stacy's dad and her mom turned toward her.

"Hi. Orchid asked me to come to the house." Christie strode over to the well-dressed woman. It was Stacy's mother. From the pictures she'd seen, Christie noted that Stacy had been a younger version of the woman. A smooth forehead and tight jawline let Christie know that she cared about her appearance and wanted to stave off the signs of aging.

She held out her hand to the woman. "I'm Christie. I'm so sorry about your daughter."

The woman swiveled away from Christie, her shoulders shaking with emotion. When she'd composed herself, she turned back. "I'm Irene Fredrich."

It seemed strange to say nice to meet you in such circumstances, so Christie nodded before turning toward Stacy's dad. "Any more news?"

"Nothing yet. But they tell me they're working on it."

"Well, just so you know. We want to see your daughter receive justice. And for you all to have some closure in this."

Irene patted her eyes, dark mascara smeared underneath. "Thank you. It's been just horrible not knowing if the police are making any progress."

"Well, even in things this old, new advances in technology and forensics have helped capture many, um, people." She hadn't wanted to say the word, killers, in case it caused more anguish for Stacy's parents.

"True, but think about it. Even with DNA advances, it doesn't help. We had lots of parties here in this backyard over the years and, of course, our DNA is all over everything. Unless someone is caught outright, I don't see how the police are going to fix this." She held a fist up to her mouth, stopping herself from saying more. Tears sprung to her eyes as she shook her head in dismay. "I can't take this. I can't take not knowing."

"That's why we're working through the list of suspects."

"You are?" Stacy's father asked, glancing over at Irene. He stepped toward her and lightly laid his hand on her shoulder. Even though they had been apart for so many years, the gesture spoke of his love for her.

"Yes, I've spoken to her boyfriend, Dwight."

"I doubt you'll get anything coherent out of him. He's a drunk."

Christie continued, "And to Donna."

Stacy's mom composed herself before asking, "I remember Donna. Did she offer any insight?"

"No. I think she thought we were accusing her of being involved."

She shrugged. "Could be. Anything else?"

"We didn't speak to him, but Dwight told us that the coach may have been involved with kids back in the day. However, he's now locked up for assault and murder. There's definitely motive if he felt he was going to lose his job or worse. And as we see, he's capable. It would just be if he would admit to it. It would only add on more time so not sure it would benefit him to confess if he had any involvement."

Irene snapped, "Exactly. I can see him doing it. He was an awful man. I never liked him."

Stacy's father glanced over at the woman, a strange expression on his face. He sighed. "True. They may never get to the truth. And that's something we'll have to live with. But at least now we can bury our daughter properly."

"Orchid said you're going to have a small gathering?"

"Yes, we don't want it to turn into a circus for the media, and we don't want anyone to know where she's buried. At least for now."

"That's understandable." She turned as Orchid came around the corner.

"Hello. Do you all want to come inside?"

"No. We just stopped by to—" His shoulders shook, and he stopped to calm himself. "We put this gazebo up for Stacy, and we want to have it rebuilt."

Her mother finished his thoughts. "I think we

saw everything we needed to see."

"Okay. Well, if there's nothing else—" Orchid replied.

Irene paused, "Oh, I forgot. I have some boxes I stored up in the attic. I'll come by and get them later if that works for you. Tomorrow or the next day?"

"That should work. Would you like us to get them down for you?" Orchid responded.

"Um, sure. That would be nice if you don't mind. Then I can just put them in my car." Irene smiled, but it didn't reach her eyes.

"Christie, can you help me with that?"

"Yes, be happy to help."

They said their goodbyes, and the pair went around to the front door. As Orchid unlocked the door, Christie glanced over at the tree. A makeshift shrine had been set up, and the ground was dotted with flowers, cards, and teddy bears. Even a large football mum with all the ribbons had been placed there.

Orchid moaned. "See? It's already starting. How long will this house be known as the place they found those dead kids? It feels oppressive here now."

"But Orchid, where will you go? Please don't say you're moving."

Orchid looked up at Christie. "Honey, sometimes life puts things in our path, and we have to follow where it leads. Right now, I've only got a glimpse of it."

Christie hated it when Orchid spoke in riddles. Orchid unlocked the door, and they went inside. The front room was bare, so unlike Orchid to not have some type of art installation. "Should I get those boxes down while we're thinking about it?"

"Probably a good idea." They went into the hallway, where a string hung down from the opening to the attic. She pulled at it, the trapdoor opening to reveal a set of stairs. Unfolding them, she climbed up and popped her head into the attic. There were a few boxes that were marked Christmas and as she looked around, she saw the boxes belonging to Stacy's mother. Reaching over, she thought better of it and called down to Orchid.

"Do you have a pair of gloves, an old towel or something I can use to grab these boxes? They're pretty dusty, and I don't want to encounter any brown recluses."

Orchid shouted up to her. "Sure. Let me go get some gloves from the garage."

Christie backed down the staircase, resting her back against the hall wall. Orchid brought over some heavy gardening gloves and Christie could grab the boxes with only a few spiderwebs attached. Setting them down in the front room, she set the gloves on top of the boxes.

Orchid looked up from her phone. "That was Lily. Are you ready to head out to dinner?"

"Yes, let me wash my hands first."

Christie followed Orchid over to the hotel where they collected Lily. Then Christie drove them down to the Riverwalk. They enjoyed the boat ride and sharing a huge platter of various fajitas at the Bare Reptile. When she dropped them off much later, Christie was glad that she didn't have to get up early for work the next morning. After last night's poor sleep, she fell into bed, snuggling up to her pillow.

A text message dinged.

Nooo. She reached over and looked at it. It was from Lana.

Got a call from Donna. Let's talk tomorrow about what she said.

Christie typed K, setting the phone down. She punched her pillow again before losing herself to a deep sleep.

She sniffed. Her nose twitched.

What is that?

Christie bolted up in bed.

Fire!

CHAPTER NINETEEN

Christie threw back the covers. The smell was growing stronger now. She rushed into the living room where she could see light outside. Going out on the deck, she spied the wooden steps leading up to her house were on fire. She heard a groan as the bottom post burst into flame, collapsing.

She couldn't go down the main stairs. That meant she was trapped. She'd been admonished about not having another way down, but she'd planning on adding an elevator for when she got older. And she'd planned on buying a ladder for her upstairs window. It had been on her list of things to do, but she still hadn't gotten around to it.

She laughed hysterically as the thought of the headline, 'Procrastination Kills. Woman dies because of not completing her to-do list.' She could tell that panic was setting in. She forced herself to take five deep breaths to calm her system. Running back to her backroom, she rang

Pop.

"Pop. Can't talk. Call the fire department!" She hung up, not wanting to tie up the line in case she needed it.

She went to the bathroom and threw towels into the tub, where she wet them down. Running back to the front room, she saw that just putting it by the door wouldn't matter. She went back into her room, stuffing the towels at the bottom of the bedroom door to give her some time before the smoke reached her.

She opened the window in her bathroom and climbed out on the walk that went around her house. Could she tie bed sheets to the outer posts? Then she looked down. There sat the trampoline. She heard glass break in the other room.

"Here goes nothing."

She jumped.

It catapulted her into the air, but she kept her head and came down in a sitting position. She needed to stop the motion as quick as possible. A few more bounces should slow it down enough. On the last one, she caught the side of the trampoline, sending her over onto the hard, rocky ground.

Landing hard on her back, the air was knocked out of her. She tried to remain calm. In a moment, she was able to catch her breath. Gingerly, she rose on her knees, brushing off the pebbles as she winced when she felt the tender burn and scraps along her arm. It was red and raw from landing on that side. She made it to her feet, backing away from the house. Headlights found her, and Pop rushed out of his truck.

A child again, she ran into her father's arms. "Oh, Pop." The tears fell, and she struggled against huge sobs.

"There, there now. I'm here. Everything's going to be all right. Don't you fret none." He stroked her back.

"But my house."

"Houses can be rebuilt."

They turned as the volunteer fire department trucks raced down their road. She saw Bryson's truck following behind. As one of the volunteers, he would have been notified as well. He pulled off to the side, running toward her, fear and worry on his face.

"Are you okay?" He gathered her up in his arms. "You're shaking."

"I'm going into shock, I think." Christie replied.

"Ever the nurse. Come on. Let's get you checked out." He soothed her.

EMTs met her, and they escorted her to the back of the vehicle.

Tears slid down her cheeks as she watched her home, now totally engulfed. Even when they put the fire out, it wouldn't be habitable.

What had caused the fire? There had been no rain or lightning. She'd been careful about clearing off any brush so that her house had a good barrier in case of fire. She'd chosen cob as it was fire resistant and the base had been changed from wood to concrete. But once the fire had gained a foothold, it had still been unstoppable.

It wasn't long before the fire was under control. Bryson walked over to the crew, and Christie could see them speaking in hushed voices. They walked over, and she saw them all gathered around one spot. She sought to rise and go join them, but the medical technician was still working on cleaning her scraped knees and shins. She winced as the pain roared to life.

Bryson nodded and then walked over to her. His brow was furrowed.

"What is it?"

"They aren't going to make any comments, but it looks like arson."

"Arson!"

"Yes, someone intentionally set that fire. Did you hear anything last night?"

"No, but I was so tired that I—wait. I remember thinking I heard bees buzzing." She gasped. "A motorcycle maybe?"

"Looks like I need to have a word with Dwight. Now, let's get you over to your dad's house. Is there anything I can do or get you right now?"

She stared at the smoldering remains of her house. Tears fell, and her shoulders shook with emotion. "Yes. There is something you can do.

Hold me."

~~

When Christie woke, she felt the pain in her body from her fall off the trampoline. Her hands, arms, and legs bore gauze from the administrations of the medical tech. She eased over on her side. Her head ached, and her eyes were puffy from the smoke and tears. Her throat and chest hurt too. She must have inhaled more smoke than she'd realized.

Christie heard voices in the other room. She eased herself up, sitting on the edge of the bed. Taking in a deep breath, she rose, feeling the aches and pains of her muscles.

She walked to the bathroom, splashing water on her face. The woman staring back at her showed the signs of pain and grief. One side appeared to have a bit of sunburn. The heat from the fire must have caught up to her as she jumped.

She smoothed her hair back and hobbled into the kitchen. Pop rose to greet her. "Oh, darlin, my heart aches to see ya like this."

"I'm okay, Pop. A little sore, but I'll be okay."

Lana was pulling a casserole from the oven. "Here, are you hungry?"

"No, I think I'll wait for lunch."

"Hun, lunch is long over. It's past supper now."

Christie hadn't even noticed that it was dark outside. She slumped into a chair Bryson pulled out for her. Another man was sitting at the table. She recognized him from last night. Must be one of the firefighters.

Bryson moved back to his place. "Would you like some iced tea or coffee?"

"Coffee would be great. Plus some water and aspirin, please."

"Your wish is my command." He poured coffee while Pop went off to grab the aspirin.

"I'm sorry. I don't think we've met. Thank you for all the work you do. And please give my thanks to all the other volunteers."

"You're welcome. Just curious. Did you put that trampoline there on purpose for just such an instance?"

"No, it was a recent gift."

Lana plopped a plate down with a helping of hamburger casserole and some salad. Christie stared at it before taking a bite and then another.

"I just felt led to get it and put it there until Christie could decide where she wanted it."

"Well, that gift may have saved her life."

"I've always heard that if you feel led to do something, you should do it."

"Even if it means asking someone you don't know out to dinner?"

Christie stopped midway through bringing the fork to her mouth. Had he just asked Lana on a date?

Lana smiled. "Yes. I think so."

"When would be a good time to ask?"

Christie set her fork down. "Oh, stop it. He's asking you out, do you want to go out with him?"

"Yes, I think that would be nice."

He rose. "Well, I need to get going for now, but if you'll walk me out, I'll get your phone number, and we can set up a time."

"Fine."

They left the kitchen and Christie shook her

head from side to side, forgetting about her headache. She moaned, "Pop, you got those aspirin?"

He handed her the bottle. She popped the pills in her mouth before swigging down the water behind them. Lana returned.

"If that don't beat all? My house burns down, I almost become a cooked turkey, and you get a date out of the deal."

Lana laughed. "God works in mysterious ways."

CHAPTER TWENTY

"If y'all will excuse me, I'm going back to bed." She rose gingerly.

Bryson walked over and helped her to the room. At the door, she laid her head on his chest and wept. He simply stroked her hair, whispering, "It will be all right."

She sniffed, looking up into his caring eyes. "I know it will. And partly because of you. I feel safe and know that you're telling me the truth. Today not so much but tomorrow or the day after, I can start thinking about what's next. But I know one thing now and I don't need to think about it."

"What?"

"I want us to get married sooner rather than later. What would you think about that?"

"I think that sounds perfect. But just to make sure that isn't the pain or the pain pills talking, how about we wait and discuss it tomorrow?"

"I doubt aspirin counts as pain pills."

"Those weren't aspirin. Pop called into town

and spoke with the doc. He ordered a prescription after checking with the techs who treated you."

Anger bristled in her chest. "I can't believe—"

"Your Pop loves you. We all do. We also know that you'll suffer through instead of getting the rest you need to recover and heal."

Christie wiped the tears from her cheeks. "See, I told you I need you. It's hard letting go of being independent. I've done it for so long. Here I moved back to Comfort to take care of Pop, only for him to be the one caring for me."

"No one's keeping score. It's what families do. It's what friends do." He hesitated. "It's what husbands do." He kissed her lightly on the lips. "Now, let's get you into bed, and don't worry about getting up at any time. I've already spoken to Lana, and she said if you even try to drive over to the rescue, you'll be turned away before you even get out of the truck. She said to let you know she has it in hand, and she doesn't want to see your face all week."

"All week?"

He cocked his head, raising his brows. "All

week. Understood?"

"Yes, understood." She made a pretend salute, groaning as pain shot through her arm.

"Now, come on. You get in the bed, and I'll see you tomorrow." He brushed his lips against her forehead as he helped her into bed. "Only sweet dreams, okay?"

"I'll try." She smiled up at him, her eyes fighting to stay open. The last words she heard as she drifted off were, "As for me, I'll find out who did this."

~~

When Christie woke again, it was late afternoon. She had slept for over twelve hours. A glass of water was next to her bed, and on the chair across the room she saw a pile of clean clothing. She cleared her throat, not realizing how raw it was until now. She sat up in bed and took a drink of water as a knock sounded on the doorjamb.

"Hello there." It was Lana.

"Lana! Who's minding the shop?"

"Don't worry. It's all in hand. I called the

board, and they all came over to help out. Seems like they feel it takes all of them to do your job." She laughed.

"Well, if nothing else, I guess it's job security." She gritted her teeth as she adjusted her position.

"Do you need some more aspirin?"

She made a face at Lana. "Bryson told me about the 'aspirin', so no, I don't want any or who knows how long I'll sleep next time."

"Would you have willingly taken them, or would you have tried to power through the pain?'

"Well, I—" She moaned as she repositioned herself.

"See? We only did it for your own good."

"I know. Bryson told me. I feel useless here, and—" Tears welled up.

"If you want, I'll come and take you over to the house later today. Right now they're sifting through it to see what can be salvaged."

Tears slid down Christie's cheeks. "I don't know why I'm so emotional. It's just a building, really. And stuff. So many people are going through so much more than I have."

"Just because others are dealing with tragedy doesn't negate yours or your feelings. It's only human to feel loss. Especially when it wasn't 'just a building.' It was your home."

"Lana, I have something very important to ask you."

Her brows furrowed, "Yes?"

"Will you be my maid of honor?"

"Are you kidding! Of course I will." Lana hugged Christie, who yelped at the pain when the movement jarred her body.

"Oh, sorry. I forgot. Also, I've been instructed to let you know that you have an appointment tomorrow morning with the doctor. His exact words were 'No if's, ands, or buts. And no telling me she doesn't need to see me, as she can nurse her own wounds.'"

"Ugh, how come so many people know me too well?"

Lana sat on the edge of the bed, "He said that nurses and doctors are the worst for going to see someone. Now, are you hungry? If you want, I can run you a bath, oh wait, he said, no bath. Shower, then. And I can make you something to eat. How does eggs, grits, and biscuits sound?"

"It sounds perfect. But if I shower, I'm going to need some more gauze and tape or bandages."

"Already done. Plus, there's some ointment for the scrapes and burns."

"Burns? Did I get burned?"

"One side got a bit of what might be called a nasty sunburn. And a bit on your feet and hands. You know you're not supposed to go back into a home when it's on fire."

"I didn't ... okay, I thought if I put a wet towel in front of the door, it might keep some of the smoke out."

"You were lucky, as you could have been caught up in there." She admonished Christie.

"You're right. It was a stupid move. I, to be honest, I wasn't thinking very well."

"Understandable. Now, can you make it to the bathroom on your own, or do you need help?"

"If you can help me up from the bed, I think I can do the rest on my own." Christie slid her bandaged legs over the edge, groaning with the movement.

"Ready?" Lana put Christie's arm around her shoulder and around her waist.

"This is silly, I'm taller and bigger than you."

"But I'm stronger and meaner, so there's that. Now on the count of three, and if you get dizzy, let me know, and we can put you back on the bed. One, two—"

Christie stood, her legs shaking like a newborn foal. Together, they shuffled into the bathroom. Yesterday, she'd been able to do this. Must have still been out of it.

"Remember, don't try to be a superwoman. If you need my help, you call me."

Christie nodded as Lana closed the door behind her. She rested her hands on the sink, taking deep breaths before looking into the mirror. Her face was red, like she'd spent the day on the lake, but it didn't appear too bad. Taking her time to remove the bandaged areas, she saw the good work the tech had done in cleaning the areas.

After she'd removed her clothes, she stepped

into the shower, being careful to avoid direct spray on her forearms and shins. Washing her hair was another chore, as lifting her arms seemed to be an impossible task, so she finally bent over and did it that way. After letting the warm water run down her head and back, she reluctantly stepped from the bath, wrapping a big fluffy bath towel around her. These weren't Pop's, so Lana must have brought them when she came over. She put her hair up into another towel and sat down on the toilet to apply medicinal ointment to her legs. By the time they were bandaged, she heard Lana at the door.

"Okay in there?"

"Yes, just a bit slower than usual."

"It's fine. How do you want your eggs and how many?"

Christie's stomach grumbled. "Three. Scrambled, I think."

"And coffee?"

"Oh, yes." She went to work on her arms. Once those were bandaged, she dressed into the clothes Lana had set on a hamper. She applied lotion to her face and brushed her teeth. Sighing, she allowed the simple act of taking a shower and brushing her teeth to remind her of simple blessings.

When she made it out to the table, Lana looked up from the stove. "Hey, you. Bryson is on his way over. Do you want to leave your hair up in a towel, or—"

"Oh, I totally forgot."

"Here, let me help." They went back to the bathroom, where Lana ran a comb through Christie's hair and then put it up into a bun. "Better?"

"Yes. You know, when I was nursing, people would say thank you for helping them do these things. I never realized how these simple things can mean so much when you can't do them."

"I'm sure you were a blessing to all the people you cared for over the years."

"Well, I know that you're a blessing in my life. I might have come out a lot worse if that silly trampoline hadn't been there. I may have been dealing with broken bones, or worse. Thank you for listening to that nudging to do it."

"You're welcome. Now, let me pour you a coffee, and I'll start the eggs. I didn't want them to get cold while you were in the shower."

Christie eased into a chair while Lana cracked eggs into a bowl. She added salt, pepper, and a dash of whipping cream. As she poured the beaten mixture into the hot buttered iron skillet, they heard Bryson's voice.

He entered the room. "Um, something smells good."

"Biscuits, grits, and eggs."

"Yum." He took a seat next to Christie. "How are you feeling this morning?"

"Better. Any news on the house?" She looked at his face as he pursed his mouth. "Tell me the truth."

"They don't think it can be fixed. They're going to mark it as a total loss."

"I figured as much. Ah well, it is what it is."

"Listen, I know that you don't want to live in town, and my place in Boerne is even farther away. Pop says that if you're open to it, we could build a new place over by the back kitchen. But to take your time and think about it."

"I will. You're right. As long as Pop's around, I want to be close. And that could be a good compromise, as I'd be a lot closer and could use that when I make pies."

Lana set the eggs down on the table, and the trio dug into the hot food.

"Thanks for this. I was hungry. I missed breakfast this morning."

Christie stared at Bryson. "What aren't you telling me? Or avoiding telling me?"

"Boy, you already know me too well." He wiped his mouth and set his fork on his plate. "Because you thought you might have heard a motorcycle, I went to have a little chat with Dwight" He took in a deep breath.

"And?"

"He's dead. I found him and his bike off the road."

CHAPTER TWENTY ONE

"What happened?"

"Probably drunk. Looks like he must have hit something, and who knows, maybe he over-corrected?"

Christie sat back in her chair. Tears threatening again. How long would these emotions be so intense? "Great, another dead end."

"Are you sure you heard a motorcycle outside your house?"

"I don't know if it was outside of my house. I just remember hearing it speed up. It could have been out on the road."

Lana set the food on the table before pouring coffee for everyone.

Bryson pulled apart a biscuit, smearing it with butter and honey. "Well, if he set the fire, it makes sense. Though I'm not sure why he'd do it. But alcohol can make you do stupid things. Maybe he didn't want you nosing around anymore."

"Why didn't you tell me about him?"

Bryson replied, "You already had enough to deal with over the last few days without adding that to your thoughts."

"So he probably killed Stacy and the young man they found with her?"

"Wait, what? Did I miss something else?" Christie asked.

"Yes, it's in the news. They did one of those forensic facial reconstructions. They believe he was around twenty and of Hispanic descent."

Christie wrapped her hands around her mug. "Then he wouldn't have been part of the high school group. What was he doing with Stacy?"

"Or maybe the question we should be asking is, what was Stacy doing with him?"

~~

With Dwight dead, this could mean they'd never know the truth about what really happened. After Bryson left, Christie went back to bed and napped for a while before sitting up in bed. She heard the television on in the next room, so Pop was back from his earlier trip to town and probably snoozing. She didn't want to wake him, so she stayed where she was.

More questions came to mind. If Dwight had come out to the property, he had to have been quieter, as she would have heard his bike if he'd been near her house. So he must have parked the bike, and then walked up to the house. From what Bryson said, the bottle with gasoline may not have destroyed the house as it was thrown aways from the house. The problem was that it had been so dry that it quickly caught and sparks hit the wooden staircase. The cob was fire resistant but not fireproof. And once the wood had been engulfed, the structure never had a chance.

She spoke aloud. "So maybe a warning to back off." She walked through it in her mind. If he had come over, thrown the bottle, he would have booked it back to where he had his motorcycle. From there, he sped off. But he had driven these roads forever and knew them like the back of his hand. Even if he drank, had he been drunk when the accident occurred? He has bound to have built up tolerance. No, something seemed off.

Or had he seen something and been taken out? No. That didn't make sense because it was late at night. Unless he was meeting someone. She picked up her phone and called the Sheriff.

"Hi, Christie. Was really sorry to hear about your house. But we'll sort this out."

"Thanks. I'm actually calling on another matter."

"Yes?"

"I heard that Dwight was killed in a motorcycle accident."

"That's correct. Must have hit a patch of gravel. He was going at a high speed when the crash occurred. I'd say the adage of don't drink and drive, but in this case, I think he probably hit something and overcorrected."

"I'd agree, but Dwight has driven these roads forever. He knows that deer cross that road at night. Doesn't it seem strange he'd be going that fast?"

"Who knows what goes through people's minds when they've been drinking?"

"How do you know he'd been drinking? Have

they already run tests?"

"No, but the deputy said he reeked of beer on his clothes."

Christie sat forward. "On his clothes? That doesn't seem right. Did you find any alcohol nearby?"

"No. But we figured that's what he used to start your house on fire. Call coming in. Gotta run. Take care."

The line went dead.

Something just didn't add up. She laid back down on the pillow, and soon sleep overtook her again. When she woke, a soft light was streaming through her window. Maybe her body was getting back to regular time. She stretched to get the kinks out. After taking another shower to loosen the kinks, she set to rebandaging her wounds. After finishing, she shuffled to the kitchen. Pop was at the sink, making coffee.

"Mornin', girlie. How ya feeling?"

"Much better, Pop." She kissed his sparse hair before taking a seat. Her phone blinked with a text message. It was from Orchid.

Stay with me today. I can come get you. I'm back at the house.

It would be nice to get away for a bit. "Pop, I think I'll drive into town and see Orchid."

"Nope. Ain't happening. Doc's orders. He wants you to go see him this morning, and no driving until he looks at ya."

Shoot, she'd forgotten about the doctor's appointment.

"I'll take you to the doc and then over to Orchid's. You can call me to come get ya when you're ready to come home."

"Thanks Pop. I hate to put you out."

He shook his head. "Not putting me out to care for my own daughter. We should get going soon."

"Okay. Hold on." The phone rang. It was the sheriff.

"Hey, Christie. I wanted to let you know that they found some beer cans along where Dwight dropped his bike."

"Cans? How could he have that?"

"Could have been carrying them in his

saddlebags."

"What's the brand?"

"Sorry?"

"The brand."

When he replied, Christie's resolve tightened in her chest. "Sheriff, check the cans for fingerprints. Because I can tell you that Dwight only drank one brand, and that wasn't it."

"What are you saying?"

"Someone wanted it to look like he was drunk when he skid out."

~~

After the doctor gave Christie the all clear, Pop dropped her off at Orchid's. Lily had stayed at the hotel and was leaving to return home later that day.

"You know what they say... We love each other, but we need a bit of space now." Orchid winked. "I'm going to make you some nettle tea, and I've also got some comfrey salve to add to your wounds. Now you put your feet up on that chaise, and I'll be right with you."

Christie laughed. "All this spoiling is going to

make me lazy."

"I very much doubt that." She moved into the kitchen.

Christie glanced over and saw the boxes they'd pulled down from the attic for Stacy's mom. "I see the boxes are still here."

She raised her voice. "Yes, they've been busy getting things planned for the service for Stacy. They've invited me to come. Would you like to join me?"

"Sure." Curiosity got the best of her, and she made her way over to the boxes. "Um, have you looked inside these?"

Orchid appeared at the entrance carrying two cups of tea. "No, I figured we'd go through them together."

Christie cracked open the box to find papers, old yearbooks, and lots of pictures in sleeves. It was so funny how photographs are handled now compared to back then. She pulled out the pictures, passing them to Orchid. They were pictures of Stacy and Donna and the other girls, and what looked like a trip to a university. A large house in the background bore Greek letters on them.

"Looks like mom was a sorority girl." Christie set the photos aside and picked up a yearbook. Sure enough, pictures of her mother with lots of other girls, grinning broadly, stared out from the picture.

Orchid interrupted Christie's thoughts, "Oh, check this out." It was a different size photo than the others. The photo was of Stacy's mom and Donna. It looked like the same background where all three of them had posed. "Check out the back."

In teenage scrawl it said, *To my other mom. You're the best! Love Donna.*

So Donna and Stacy's mom had a close relationship. Had there been jealousy between the girls? Plus, if Stacy had taken the head cheerleader spot away from Donna, would that have given Donna the motive to kill her? And if they were friends, it made sense that Stacy would have confided in Donna about the subterfuge with Dwight.

But it all came back to one thing. How were

the deaths related and who was killed first?

CHAPTER TWENTY TWO

Christie wore a new midi dress with flats. It had long sleeves so that most of the bandages were under wraps. Driving with Orchid, they made it past a guard who was watching the entrance to the event center and stopping everyone. Orchid pulled a card from her purse and showed it to the security guard, who waved her into the parking lot.

As they drove in, Christie noted another person walking down the main street to see if people had placed tags on their windshields. Certainly that was a public road, so they couldn't stop people from parking there. And if anyone had even gotten a hint of the event, it would make sense to see some reporters around.

Orchid parked and noticed that Stacy's parents had already arrived. Another car that looked familiar was parked next to theirs. Possibly Donna's. They met someone at the door, most likely from the event center staff, who escorted them into the entranceway.

Inside, the cathedral ceiling made the entrance appear grander. As Christie glanced up, she noticed Stacy's mother and father in what appeared to be a heated argument. Their voices were lowered, but it was evident by their faces and mannerisms that the topic was contentious. It was sad that Stacy's disappearance had destroyed what had been a happy family.

"If you'll follow me."

"Oh, sorry, I was just admiring the foyer." Christie responded before falling in behind Orchid. In the next room, a large fireplace dominated the space. Long brown tables with high-back chairs were situated around the room. Pitchers of water were placed on the table. And in the corner, they'd set up coffee and cold drinks which had captured most people's attention who milled around the room with quiet voices.

"Please, everyone, help yourself to drinks." The event manager left the room, and the mood lightened and people's voices grew louder as they came together in small circles of conversation.

While Christie didn't recognize many of the people, they looked familiar, and she realized that many were people she'd seen in Stacy's yearbook. Here were Stacy's peers. A tap on her shoulder startled her.

Christie turned to see Donna. "I'm sorry. I didn't mean to make you jump. I wanted to come over and apologize for my behavior the other day. I think it was the shock of hearing everything. But that's no excuse for my manners."

"Don't let it trouble you. We should have been more up front about our intentions instead of the way we handled it." Christie thought about what she'd heard Donna say and asked, "If you don't mind me asking, what did you mean by 'she finally did it.' I'm curious what you meant."

"Stacy had told me she was dating someone and that her parents wouldn't approve. You know how parents are. Especially those with one child. They doted on her and had big plans and dreams for her."

"Yes, I suppose every parent does to some extent. Was there a reason Stacy was the only child?"

Donna lowered her voice, and they moved toward a table when another couple entered the room. "Her mother wanted more children, but she couldn't have any more. So they put all their time and energy into Stacy. Today, they'd be called helicopter parents."

"I'd think that having your parents around would be a good thing."

"Yes, but, well, I have to be honest. I was a bit jealous of Stacy. They gave her anything she wanted. They adored her. I know my parents loved me, but I had four brothers and sisters. They only had so much time to devote to me, what with working and so many activities. Plus, the money was tight. So being in the cheerleading squad was difficult."

That made Christie remember how Stacy had ended up as head cheerleader. Was Donna saying these things now so that others would feel sorry for her?

Someone tapped the side of a glass to get people's attention. "Everyone, if you'll please take a seat, we'll begin shortly."

Donna excused herself, and Orchid rejoined Christie at the table they'd chosen. Christie had wanted to ensure that she was facing forward and not having to turn her chair. This way, she could more easily see those who had gathered.

Christie's mother and father stepped forward. Irene held a handkerchief in one hand and cleared her throat before speaking. "Thank you all for coming. This would have meant the world to Stacy." She stopped and clenched her mouth before taking a long breath. "We have a slideshow first, and then we'd love for you all to come and share any good memories of your time with Stacy. We are here to celebrate her life."

They moved over, and the slideshow began. Stacy as a baby, a young girl, and pictures that included many of the people in the room at school or church events. Later there were shots of football games, and even a shot of Dwight and Stacy at junior prom. A collective gasp went up when their picture came up on the slide. She'd been hearing people talk about his recent death.

They must have had the slideshow done earlier or decided to leave it in after his death. A bit surprising, Irene hadn't said anything about him, but she was probably more focused on Stacy.

Finally, it ended with a photo of Stacy, most likely one of her senior pictures.

When it concluded, there was silence except for the sniffles of some women. Finally, one man stood up. He was tall and a bit portly. As soon as he began to speak, everyone laughed, breaking the tension. Christie wondered if he'd been the person in high school who everyone liked and had made people laugh. With the first sentiments done, others rose. One by one they shared about Stacy and her antics or friendship. All the laughter reminded her of the time at the movies with Lana.

Her mind went back to the scene, but a simple word came spilling forward. Assume. When something is placed in front of people specifically, we simply assume it to be true. Yet appearances can be deceiving. She looked over to find Donna staring at her. She broke off eye contact, her mind thinking about what she felt was the truth. What should she do?

Finally, after the last person had spoken, Stacy's father and mother came to the front.

Irene said, "Thank you all for coming. We have some finger foods coming in, so please stay as long as you like." She turned to Stacy's father.

Mister Fredrich broke down in tears, and gazes darted around the room. Here was a broken man. "I should have done something. This is all my fault. I'm to blame for this. Poor Stacy."

"Be quiet now, Rick. This will be over soon." Irene took his arm and gestured to the man who'd spoken earlier. He helped Stacy's dad to a chair nearby.

Christie turned to Orchid. "Listen, I need to do something. Will you go along with me? I need to see how people react. Specifically, one person."

"Okay. What do you want me to do?"

"We'll just have a conversation over by the food table and let it go from there. I need it to start by Donna and her friends. Then we need to hang back and watch people leaving."

"Okay."

Christie and Orchid joined the line when the food was brought in. She lowered her head but not enough that what she said couldn't be heard. "They think that Dwight was run off the road. There was a bit of paint on the motorcycle, and they're already looking to see what type of vehicle it matches."

As a group behind them started whispering, Christie nodded toward Orchid. As they got their plates, they repeated the scene a few more times around other groups. By the time they were done, the entire group had heard what she'd said.

"This is it Orchid. Either it works or it doesn't."

They made their way outdoors and watched as Stacy's parents spoke with guests. Soon, only a few closer friends and her parents remained. Christie was getting antsy. Maybe her ruse hadn't connected with anyone.

Donna came out of the building, walking toward Stacy's parents. After saying goodbye, she hugged them before chatting with a small group of women. Another group left, and Christie watched closely. Soon, only a handful of people were left.

She pulled Orchid back into the shadows of the entrance and watched. One by one, people got into their vehicles. But only one went to the passenger side and glanced down at the front panel.

Bingo.

She held her breath and waited until the parking lot was empty. Then they made their way to Orchid's vehicle.

Once inside the car, Orchid asked, "What does this prove?"

"If nothing else, that they were involved in Dwight's death. And possibly my house fire."

Orchid steered her car out of the parking lot. "But it makes no sense.

"You're right. It doesn't. But that's why we need to do something before it's too late."

"What do you have in mind?"

CHAPTER TWENTY THREE

Arriving back at Orchid's house, Christie made a few phone calls. She then went over to the box of Stacy's mother. Digging through the photos, she spied a few pictures of Stacy with her friends. In the background, people's faces were framed as they sat in the stands. She thought back to the pictures that Suzie had supplied. She should have noticed it earlier, but hadn't.

A knock on the door brought them back to the present.

"Who do you think it is?" Orchid asked.

Christie shrugged her shoulders as Orchid walked to the front room. She returned with Stacy's dad. "Mister Fredrich, what a surprise."

"I, I'm sorry for my outburst earlier." He ran his hand through his thinning hair, and Christie noticed his breathing was labored.

"It's understandable. Carrying that for so long has to be difficult."

Their eyes met.

"Yes, it's been a burden."

Christie continued, "Think about those other parents. They don't even know what happened to their son. At least you have closure."

"Yes, there's that."

Orchid interjected, "Mister Fredrich, will you have a seat?"

He shook his head. "No, I just wanted to let you know that we'll be selling the house now. I hate to spring this on you like this. But with Irene going back to Florida, I figured I'd better let you know. Of course, you have as long as you need to find a new place and to move."

"It's understandable that you don't want to be associated with the house any longer. Hopefully, you can think of the good memories and not the bad ones."

He nodded.

"Hello?" It was Irene.

"Come in. We're back here." Orchid called out.

Irene joined them in the room. "Oh, hello." She spoke to Christie. "I heard there was a fire at your house. That's just terrible. It appears that Dwight was behind this all along."

"Yes, they think it could be related to him."

"He always was an impressionable boy. I liked him. It's sad what happened."

"As in, easy to manipulate? I gather he and Stacy had an agreement with each other."

Stacy's dad spoke. "They were good friends. But I never saw them together long term as a couple."

Orchid interjected, "Are you here for your boxes?"

Irene breathed out. "Yes, I totally forgot about those boxes. They're just some old memories."

"I hope you don't mind. I took a peek in there. You were pledged to a sorority. I always wondered what they were like. It sounds so fun."

"Oh, it was." She shared about the pledges and mentioned the events, and every time she would slow down, Christie would ask another question.

"I bet that Stacy wanted to pledge to your sorority as well."

A dark cloud passed over Irene's face. She hesitated before speaking, "Yes, I'm sure that she would have."

"So she had her heart set on college. Lots of my friends just skipped it and got married."

Stacy's mom frowned but said nothing as Christie continued. "I believe Donna pledged to your sorority."

"Yes, I put in a good word for her. She's made something of herself. Owns her own business. She's done well."

"Maybe that's what she wanted."

"What are you implying?"

"Not everyone wants the same things in life. Maybe Stacy wanted something different."

The air was now thick with tension. Christie hoped that she hadn't spoken too soon. "I can't imagine if my child chose a direction that I didn't agree with."

"Yes, wasting a life on some—" She collected herself. "It's often because of bad outside influences."

"Like the boy she was dating?"

"I didn't have to worry about Dwight. We understood one another."

Christie heard a sound from the back. "Is that why you killed him?"

Mister Fredrich rose from his chair. "I did it. I confess. I killed him. I killed them too."

Christie turned toward him. She shook her head. "No, you didn't. I said that a car had swiped his bike, and there was paint on it. Only one person looked at their car."

She faced Irene. "That was you."

"Conjecture."

"You have a funny way with words. I think that's what started bothering me."

"Whatever do you mean?" Irene crossed her arms.

"Well, I once watched a documentary, and they noted that criminals will still speak something of the truth. For instance, when we talked about the coach or Dwight, you said, 'I can see him doing it.' Not that he did it. You were trying to focus on misdirection by pointing the finger at them. And when you said that you couldn't take not knowing, it wasn't about your daughter. It was that you were worried the truth would finally come out. You were telling the truth. Just not 'the' truth."

She faced Stacy's father. "Mister Fredrich, don't you want to see justice for your daughter? For her fiancée?"

"Stop it! He was never going to marry my daughter!" Irene spat out.

"That's why you had to get rid of him. But something went wrong."

Stacy's dad's face went pale. "Mister Fredrich, please sit down. Where are your nitro tablets?"

He shook his head. "I'm so tired. Tired of all the lies. The burden. I can't live with it anymore."

Christie saw Orchid tap in some numbers on her phone. They couldn't let Irene leave. She had called the sheriff from her car, and he'd instructed them on how to proceed.

Irene screamed. "Shut up you old fool!"

"No. You be quiet. I went along with it all these years. I couldn't face the fact that I was married to a monster. I was so in love, I just refused to believe it had been anything more than an accident. But no more. I'm not long for this world, and this is all my fault. I should be dead. Not Stacy." He hung his head in his hands.

Irene's voice threatened, "I said be quiet."

A male voice spoke. It was the sheriff. A couple of other deputies entered, and one of them stationed themselves by each of the parents.

The sheriff recited the Miranda rights. "Do you want to say anything?"

Stacy's dad looked up. "I don't care what happens to me. I have to get this off my mind."

He looked at Stacy's mom, her eyes pleading with him.

"We loved Stacy. After so many tries, finally. And she was a wonderful child. So sweet and compliant. I think that's what surprised us when she started going against our wishes in high school. We knew that Dwight wasn't a real boyfriend. We just never suspected that she was hiding one from us. I think that every parent wants what's best for their child. But some can't stand it, that they can't control someone any longer."

He glanced over at Stacy's mom, who collapsed into a nearby chair, awaiting her fate.

The words so long bottled up flowed from him while Irene sat defeated. "We were having a concrete pad put in for a storage shed. That's where she met him. He was on the work crew. He'd been at the building site of our new home. I guess they hit it off. Anyway, there'd been lots of delays on our new house. They'd prepared the area, but something had come up, and they weren't able to pour the cement." He stopped and looked over at Stacy's mom. "Tell them. Or I will."

Irene wrung her hands together. "I was in her room. Cleaning."

More likely snooping, thought Christie, but stayed silent.

"And that's when I found it. A ring. Little more than a chip of a diamond. I confronted Dwight when he came over, but he said it wasn't him. That Stacy had said she and this boy were planning on running away to get married."

She stared at the floor. "I couldn't allow that

to happen. You understand, don't you?" Her voice was pleading. "I mean, she wasn't thinking straight. I just wanted him to go away. His parents were field workers, of all things. He had no money. No position. I knew if I could pay him to go away, Stacy would come around. What kind of life would she have had?"

The irony of her words must have passed over her head, thought Christie.

"I had him meet me. To talk about the slab. I offered him money. Lots of it. He refused. He said they loved each other. They would make it work."

She rose, but the sheriff motioned for her to sit back down. "I couldn't help it. Something came over me. The shovel was there, and I picked it up."

She stopped. Her gaze fixed toward the events in the past.

Stacy's dad took up the story. "I came home later and found her digging in the backyard. She'd pulled the concrete wire back and was digging underneath it. That's when I saw him. I asked her what had happened, and she said she'd lost control. It had been an accident and had hit his head. I wanted her to go to the police. It was a momentary break. Manslaughter. She hadn't meant to do it. But she threatened me if I told anyone. She'd say that I'd done it. We were so engaged with each other we hadn't known that Stacy had come home and that she'd come outside."

Stacy's mom cried out. "It was an accident. I meant to hit him." She pointed at Mister Fredrich. "Not her. Not my baby!" She broke down sobbing. "Stacy, my baby. Stacy."

The sheriff motioned to his deputy, who went over and helped Irene from her chair. He set the cuffs on her arms and moved toward her dad.

His face was pale, and Christie sprang into action. "Give me your heart pills, Mister Fredrich."

He shook his head. "I've had to live with my guilt all these years. It's true. Your sin will always find you out. Mine have. I'm tired."

"No. You can't do this."

"I can and I will." He groaned as the pain increased.

"Help, call an ambulance. He's having a heart attack."

"No. I've dishonored those two young people. My life has been nothing but hell since then."

"Because you loved your wife and wouldn't turn her in. That's why you moved out."

He nodded. "I'd already lost Stacy. It wouldn't bring her back I had the gazebo built because Stacy had always wanted one."

"A memorial to her." Christie crouched down in front of him.

He nodded. His breathing was coming faster. "I can't do anything now. I won't testify against her. She's still my wife and I won't do it."

The sounds of an ambulance approached the house. Christie rose as workers came into the room and took over treating him.

Orchid came over and hugged her. "It's over."

"Will you stay? I can't bear for you to leave."

"It may not be up to me, but we'll talk about it another time." Orchid walked away, leaving Christie realizing that sometimes you don't get all the answers you want.

CHAPTER TWENTY FOUR

The coverage of the arrest of Stacy's mom dominated the news. Her father remained in the hospital, but doctors had been instructed with do not resuscitate orders. He'd also refused surgery. It would only be a matter of time before he succumbed. So many lives destroyed.

Weeks later, a small group of people gathered on an overcast day, with a light drizzle falling as they laid two young people to rest. The headstone was a simple plaque.

Luis and Stacy Hernandez.

Her mother hadn't prevented their marriage. And her mother hadn't taken two lives, but three. They hadn't released the information that Stacy had been pregnant. The trial, if there was one, would most likely be one of the most sensational and sensitive in Kendall county history.

Already Irene had changed her story to make it out that Stacy's father had done the killing, and she had been the one to go along with it out of fear. But he had written everything out and had it notarized in case he wasn't around. He'd also done a video testimony. Now it would be up to a jury to determine the truth.

Irene Fredrich had lawyered up, and the paint on the rental car had matched Dwight's bike. She must have asked to meet him close to their property. It was determined that she had been the one who Pop had seen sitting on their road. She had most likely cajoled Dwight into setting the fire as a warning. Like she'd said, he'd always been impressionable. All she had to say was that Christie would share the truth about him and Stacy.

However, in reality, Irene had not simply wanted to warn Christie. She'd wanted to place the blame on Dwight. When he got on his bike, she followed him and ran him off the road. She wanted to make it appear that Dwight had been the killer all along. They may not get her for the two earlier deaths, but she had made a mistake this time. She would be going to prison for the rest of her life.

Christie watched as Luis's parents were consoled by other children. Thankfully, they would at least know what happened. As the mourners left, Christie felt the rain on her head. Even the day seemed to be crying.

Loss came in so many forms. The loss of a dream. The loss of a person. The loss of trust. She sighed and felt a firm hand close over hers.

"Are you ready to go home?"

She had no house, and it would be months before they built another one. But she knew that home wasn't a building or a dwelling, it was a place in your heart. It was the people you surrounded yourself with every day. Who loved you unconditionally. She turned to Bryson.

"Yes. I'm ready."

~~

A Note From the Author

If you enjoyed Death Wakes A Snake, please leave a review. It helps other readers to know if they would also enjoy this type of mystery. Did you figure out the killer? If you want to read a more light-hearted mystery, you can get Sleuths at the Spa by signing up for my newsletter. In my newsletter, I keep you up to date on what I'm working on, discounts and sales, as well as sharing other authors' books with you. I'd love to connect, so sign up and receive a free mystery. https://www.vikkiwalton.com/newsletter/

Also a big thanks to Susan Furtado who allowed me to create a character around her.

Apricot Fried Pies Recipe

Apricot Compote

3 lbs. apricots

¼ to ½ cup sugar (dependent on sweetness desired)

1 ½ tsp vanilla

1 TBS lemon juice

½ cup cold water

Cut the apricots up into slices or bite-sized pieces.

Combine the sugar, water, and juice in a heavy saucepan. Add in the apricots and cook on low until the apricots break apart. If desired, you can blend with an immersion blender if you don't want chunks in your compote.

You can make the compote ahead of time and have it in the fridge or freezer before making the fried pies.

Fried Pie Dough

For the quick method:

Use a can of prepared biscuits. For larger biscuits, either make larger pies or divide them in half. Using a roller, create a circle. Add the compote to one side. Fold the other side over the compote, and crimp the edges with a fork, ensuring that the compote remains inside.

Fry in hot oil until brown and golden. Dry on a rack or over paper towels to absorb the grease.

If desired, when cool, you can dust it with powdered sugar (optional).

Serve warm with vanilla ice cream or eat cold.

You can also use prepared pie crust. Unroll the pie crust, cut out circles and add the compote as before.

Standard pie dough recipe:

2 ½ cup all-purpose flour

¾ TBS salt

1 stick unsalted butter (chilled and cut into small pieces)

2 ½ TBSP shortening or lard (also chilled and cut into small pieces)

5 TBSP ice cold water

2 TBSP sugar

Combine the flour, salt, and sugar. Working in batches, work in the cold butter and shortening into the flour mixture. Add water as you go.

Don't over mix the dough. When the butter/shortening is integrated, wrap in plastic and place in the fridge until needed. A minimum of thirty minutes to a few hours, or overnight.

When ready to create the pies, unwrap and divide the dough, making small circles to the size desired for the fried pies. A small bowl may be used as a guide for medium to large pies.

Fill with apricot compote or other desired fruit filling.

Enjoy!